LOONEY TUNES

GREATEST HITS

VOLUME 2 YOU'RE DESPICABLE!

LOONEY TUNES GREATEST HITS VOLUME 2: YOU'RE DESPICABLE!

DC Comics, 2900 West Alameda Ave., Burbank, CA 91505
Printed by LSC Communications, Owensville, MO, USA. 2/17/17. First Printing.
ISBN: 978-1-4012-6594-6

Library of Congress Cataloging-in-Publication Data is available.

DCC039085

PEFC Certified
Printed on paper from sustainably managed forests, controlled sources
www.pefc.org

HAT
TRICK
WB1545

POOF!

POOF!

FWIP!

FWIP!

FWOOOOSH!

FLIP!

POP!

FLIP!

POP!

GLUG
GLUG

SPLOOSH!

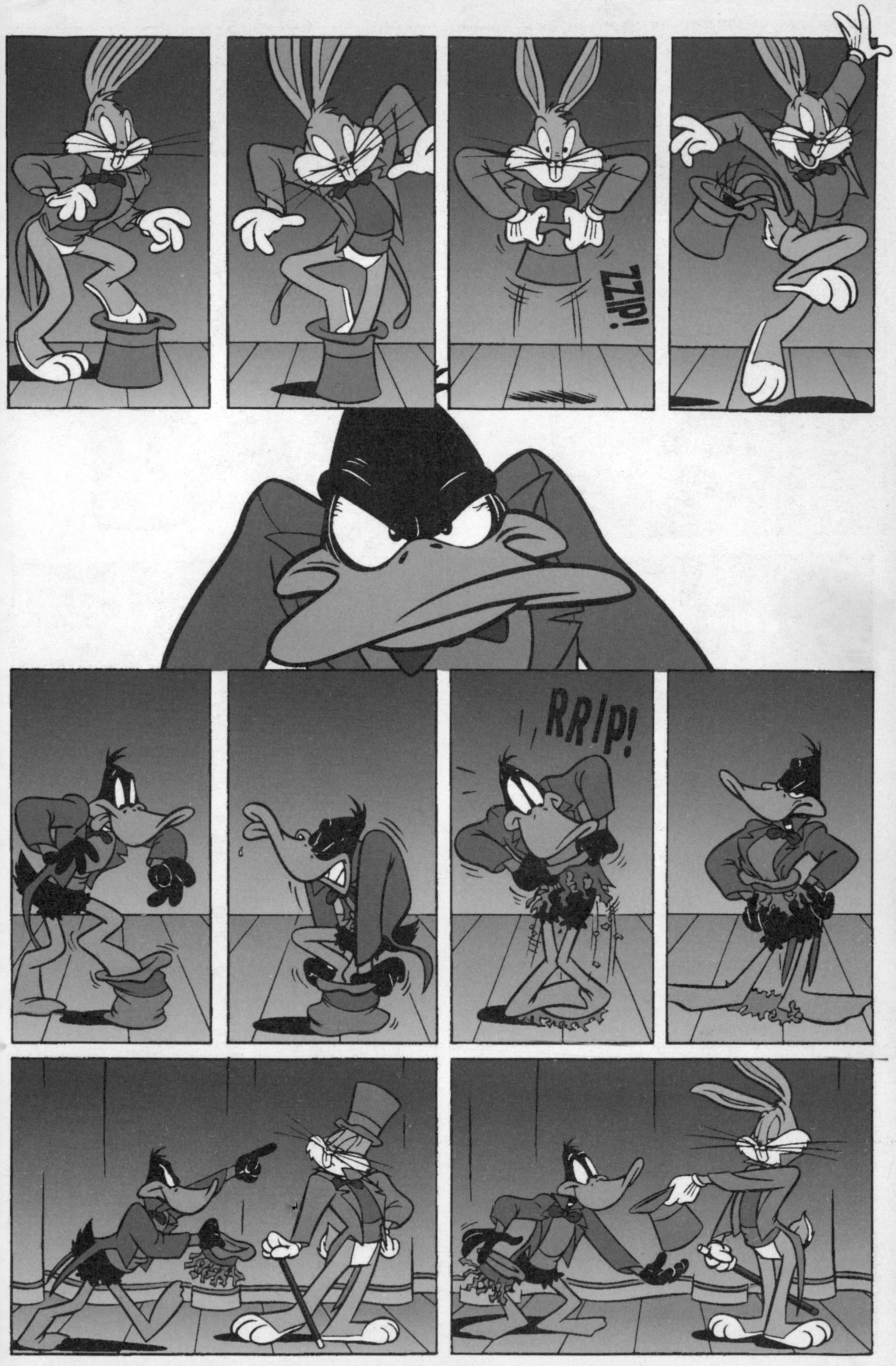
ZZIP!
RRIP!

!

FWIP!

FWIP!

THAT'S ALL FOLKS!

MANKIND, ALWAYS SEARCHING OUTWARDS FROM ITS HUMBLE HOME...

...REACHING OUT ACROSS THE VAST, EMPTY DISTANCES OF SPACE...

...EVER HOPING THAT WE WILL FIND OTHERS IN THE COSMIC WILDERNESS...

WHUMPFF!

...ALWAYS STRIVING TO FIND SIGNS OF INTELLIGENT LIFE WITH WHOM WE CAN SHARE OUR UNIVERSE!

Writer: Dave King Penciller: Nelson Luty (Sol Studio) Inker: Horacio Ottolini Letterer: John Costanza Colorist: Prismacolor

WHIMPER!

WHIZZZ
THWACK!
YIPE!

WHIRR!
WHIRR!

WHIRRR!
WHIRR!

GRRRROWL!

WHIRR!

WHIRRR!
EEK!!

WHIRRR!
WHIRR!

FFWHOOOOSH!!!

WHIMPER!

AND SO, THE LONG AWAITED QUESTION OF WHETHER OR NOT MAN IS ALONE IN THE UNIVERSE IS ABOUT TO BE ANSWERED...

...EVEN IF IT IS ONLY WITH A BARK!
ARF!
THAT'S ALL FOLKS!

ACCORDING TO COMPANY POLICY, ALL MICE WHO TRETHPASS IN THE CHEESE LAB WILL BE FILLETED, DIPPED IN BATTER, AND DEEP FRIED!
WHOOSH!
I AM NOT TRESPASSING. THIS IS OFFICIAL BEESINESS!
WHOOOOSH!
I AM HERE TO REMIND YOU TO WEAR A **HARD HAT** WHILE IN THE FACTORY!

WB1523

GATO EL HOTTO

BECAUSE THESE ON-THE-JOB INJURIES, THEY CAN BE MOST PAINFUL, NO?
OOOOF!
WHAM!

Writer: Bill Matheny Penciller: Horacio Saavedra Inker: Ruben Torreiro Letterer: Javier Saavedra Colorist: Prismacolor

TSK, TSK. EET MAY BE **DAMAGED**, BUT I KNOW MANY CHEESE EXPERTS WHO WILL BE HAPPY TO **INSPECT** IT, MY GATO MUCHACHO!

THEY ARE WAITING NOW TO START SLICING, SHREDDING, AND SPRINKLING IT OVER THEIR TAMALES! I WILL LET YOU KNOW WHAT THEY SAY! ARRIBA!

THANKS. I APPRECIATE THAT.

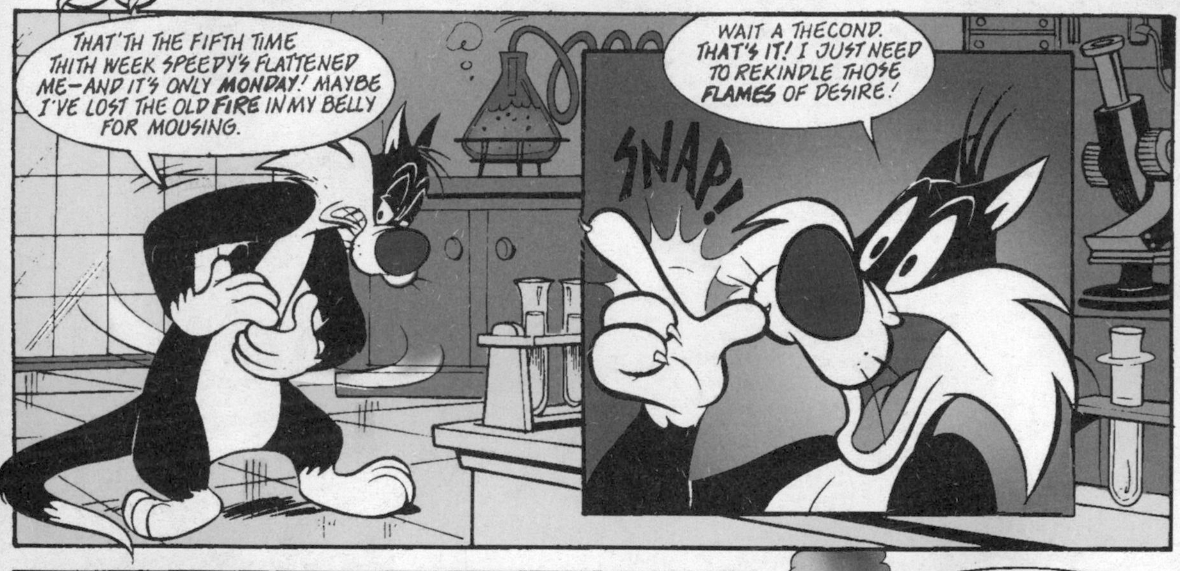

YEEE-OWWWW!
WHOOSH!
SOMETHING'S HAPPENED TO ME! BUT I GOTTA ADMIT- I LOOK GREAT IN RED!
THUFFERIN' THUCCOTASH! LOOK AT ME! I'M A FLAME-BREATHIN' THPEEDTHTER! THERE'LL BE A HOT TIME IN THE OLD CHEESE FACTORY TONIGHT!
AT THE CHEESE FESTIVAL...
WHAT WILL WE DO, SPEEDY? EET IS TERRIBLE!
JOSÉ ATE ALL THE CHEESE!
GULP! I AM SO SORRY...BECAUSE I AM STILL HUNGRY! BURP!
DO NOT WORRY. I WILL GET SOME MORE CHEESE WHILE JOSÉ'S STOMACH SETTLES!

A FEW MOMENTS LATER...
WITH JOSÉ AROUND, EET IS A GOOD THING WE HAVE CHEESE TO SPARE!
HOLY FRIJOLE! WHAT HAPPENED TO YOU, MY PUSSYCAT MUCHACHO?!
YOU CHEESE THIEVES HAVE BEEN GETTING OFF EASY SO I DETHIDED TO TURN UP THE HEAT ON YOU!
LET'TH SEE. WE CAN DO THIS THE HARD-BOILED WAY OR WE CAN DO IT THE OVER EASTHY SHOW!
YOU HAD BETTER SLOW DOWN, HOTTO EL GATO...
...BECAUSE YOU MUST BEWARE OF FALLING CHEESE!
WHAM!
YOU'LL HAVE TO DO BETTER THAN THAT, MOUSE, CAUTHE I'M LIVING LARGE AND HOT-THAUCE CHARGED!

THIS WILL GIVE YOU A LEEFT, SEÑOR GATO!
WATCH OUT FOR THUDDEN THTOPS, RODENT!
ERT
FWOOSH
GL-DONK
HOLY MUCHO FRIJOLES!
ENJOY YOUR THWIM, CHEESE-SNATCHER! YOU MIGHT EAT YOUR WAY OUTTA THAT GLOP...
...IN ABOUT FIFTY YEARS! HAR-HAR!
HATE TO RUN.. BUT I GOT A HOT DATE AT A MOUSE SMORGASBORD..
..AND I'M TH' GUEST OF HONOR!

6
>GASP< THAT EES THE FIRST TIME A CHEESE HAS TRIED TO EAT ME!
I HAVE TO GET BACK... BUT MY BELLY EES SO FULL!
PERHAPS I TAKE A LEETLE SIESTA TO DIGEST MY MEAL...
MEANWHILE, AT THE CHEESE FESTIVAL...
COME HERE, SQUIRT! I WANT AN EVEN DOZEN MOUSE-BURGERS FOR THE TABLE TONIGHT!

NOT SO FAST, GATO EL HOTTO!
BACK FOR MORE, EH? HOW'D YOU GET OUTTA THAT CHEESE ANYWAY?
SPEEECH

I AM LUCKY, SEÑOR PUSSYCAT·· I HAVE A MUY FAST METABOLISM!
WE'LL SEE ABOUT THAT ONCE I'VE RUN CIRCLES AROUND YOU!

WHAT EES WRONG? YOU NOT EVEN RUN A SEENGLE CIRCLE!
I DON'T FEEL SO GOOD.

MY 'HOT TO TROT' POTION MUST BE WEARING OFF!
STORE

DASH OF HOT THAUCE, EXTRA HOT PEPPERS, SPICY HOT SOUP...
HERE, YOU FORGOT THEES.

THANKS, RODENT!
BAKING SODA

OH, YEAH! FEEL THE BURN!
I ALWAYS DID LIKE "FAST FOOD"! HA-HA! ++URP++
YEE-HAH! I DEED NOT KNOW YOU WERE SO FESTIVE!
BURRRRRAP!
WHOOOOOSH!
KA-BOOM!
BURRRP!
BURRRP!
VIVA GATO EL HOTTO!
VIVA EL SPEEDY!
I LIKE THEE'S GATO EL HOTTO.. HE'S SILLY!
THAT'S ALL, FOLKS!

DULLES AIRPORT, WASHINGTON, D.C.
FLIGHT 1119 FROM PARIS LANDING AS FAST AS WE CAN!!!
ACME AIR
THE INVISIBLE SKUNK

SIR, YOU... *COUGH!* FORGOT YOUR NEWSPAPER.
KEEP IT!

AH... AMERICA, LAND OF ZEE FREE, HOME OF --
--ZEE MOST BEE-YOOTIFUL CREATURE EV AIR. OOH-LA-LA!
PRESIDENTIAL PET PAINTED

Writer: Michael Eury Penciller: Horacio Saavedra Inker: Ruben Torreiro Letterer: Javier Saavedra Colorist: Prismacolor

SOON, AT THE WHITE HOUSE...

NOW WHERE IS THAT BOTTLE OF DISAPPEARING INK...?

...I NEED IT TO SIGN SOME LEGISLATION I DON'T AGREE WITH.

BONJOUR, MADEMOISELLE. I AM PEPE LE PEW, FROM PAREE, ZEE CITEE OF AMOUR.

ALLOW ME TO SERENADE YOU...

"ZANK HEAVEN FOR LEETLE GURLS..."

OH, PARDON. I FORGOT, MY CHERIE IS AMERICAN. PERHAPS THEES IS A MORE APPROPRIATE SONG...

"ZEE EAST COAST GURLS ARE HEEP, I REALLY DEEG ZOSE STYLES ZAY WEAR..."
SNIFF.

HISSS!!
A GEEFT, FOR PEPE? I AM ONE LUCKY SKUNK, NO?
DISAPPEARING INK
THIS IS UNUSUAL...
SACRE BLEU! I AM AS TRANSPARENT AS MOST OF ZEE WASHEENGTON POLITICIANS!
MEOWR???

ROWWRR!
ZEE PETITE TEMPTRESS BECKONS PEPE TO FOLLOW, EH?
PEE-YOO!
PARDON MOI.
WHAT'S THAT SMELL?

MR SENATOR, SIR, DID YOU... >SNIFF< HAVE GARLIC FOR LUNCH?
EXCUSE ME?!

>SNUFF SNUFF<
I HAVE GOT TO TAKE THIS SUIT TO THE DRY CLEANER.

HOO-EEY! THERE HASN'T BEEN A STENCH LIKE THIS IN HERE SINCE THE SPEAKER OF THE HOUSE DROPPED BY!
ALLO, MADEMOISELLE.
?
YOU ARE... >SMOOCH SMOOCH< TRÈS JOLIE... >SMOOCH SMOOCH SMOOCH<
BRRRRT??
MEWWWORR!
WAIT!! YOU CANNOT ESCAPE YOUR DESTINY!
PENELOPE! COME BACK HERE, KITTY!

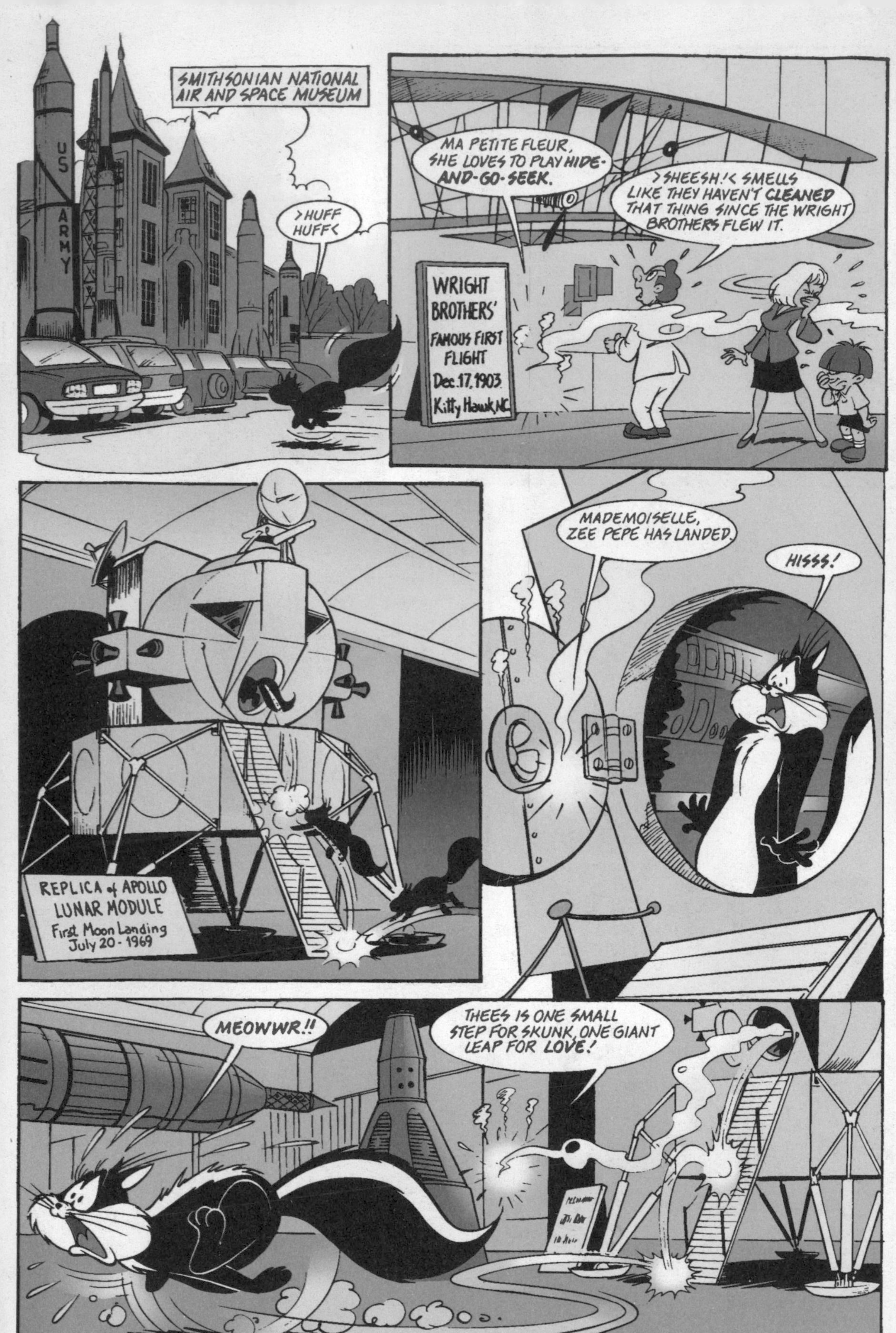
SMITHSONIAN NATIONAL AIR AND SPACE MUSEUM
US ARMY
>HUFF HUFF<
MA PETITE FLEUR, SHE LOVES TO PLAY HIDE-AND-GO-SEEK.
>SHEESH!< SMELLS LIKE THEY HAVEN'T CLEANED THAT THING SINCE THE WRIGHT BROTHERS FLEW IT.
WRIGHT BROTHERS' FAMOUS FIRST FLIGHT Dec. 17, 1903 Kitty Hawk, NC
REPLICA of APOLLO LUNAR MODULE First Moon Landing July 20 - 1969
MADEMOISELLE, ZEE PEPE HAS LANDED.
HISSS!
MEOWWR!!
THEES IS ONE SMALL STEP FOR SKUNK, ONE GIANT LEAP FOR LOVE!

SMITHSONIAN NATIONAL AIR AND SPACE MUSEUM
U.S. ARMY
>PANT! PANT!<
TOUR
WASHINGTON TOURS
..YOU GOT THE CAPITAL YOU'LL GET THE CAPITOL

WE'RE PASSING THE SMITHSONIAN MUSEUM, WHICH WE WON'T VISIT, SINCE YOU CHEAPSKATES BOOKED THE BUDGET TOUR.

NOW, ARE THERE ANY QUESTIONS?

YES. CAN YOU DIRECT ME INTO ZEE ARMS OF MY BELOVED?

UH... WHO ASKED THAT QUESTION?
ME. PEPE LE PEW, LE INVEESIBLE SKUNK.

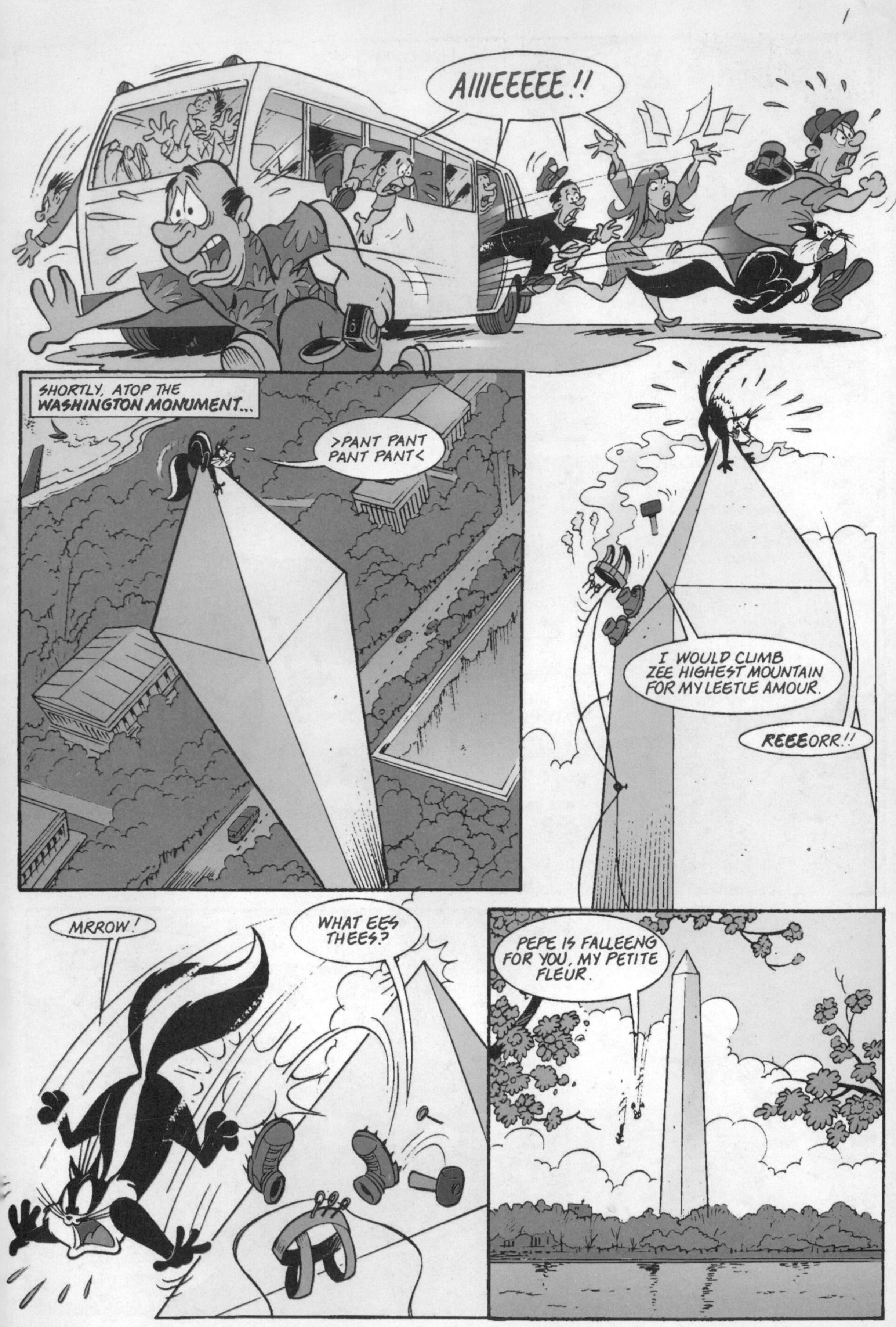
AIIIEEEEE!!
SHORTLY, ATOP THE WASHINGTON MONUMENT...
>PANT PANT PANT PANT<
I WOULD CLIMB ZEE HIGHEST MOUNTAIN FOR MY LEETLE AMOUR.
REEEORR!!
MRROW!
WHAT EES THEES?
PEPE IS FALLEENG FOR YOU, MY PETITE FLEUR.

SPLOOSSH
AH, I CAN SEE ME AGAIN. NOW, WHEN CAN I SEE YOU?
HOLD IT RIGHT HERE!
LEAVE MY CAT ALONE!
SHE IS A CAT? OOPS. MY MISTAKE.
SCREEECHH
SO TELL PEPE, WHERE DOES ONE FIND A SKUNK IN YOUR CITY?
THAT'S EASY. JUST GO TO THAT BUILDING. THERE'RE LOTS OF SKUNKS THERE-- BIG, SMELLY ONES.
MERCI! AU REVOIR! EET EES TIME FOR PEPE TO RAISE LE STEENK IN WASHINGTON, NO?
The End

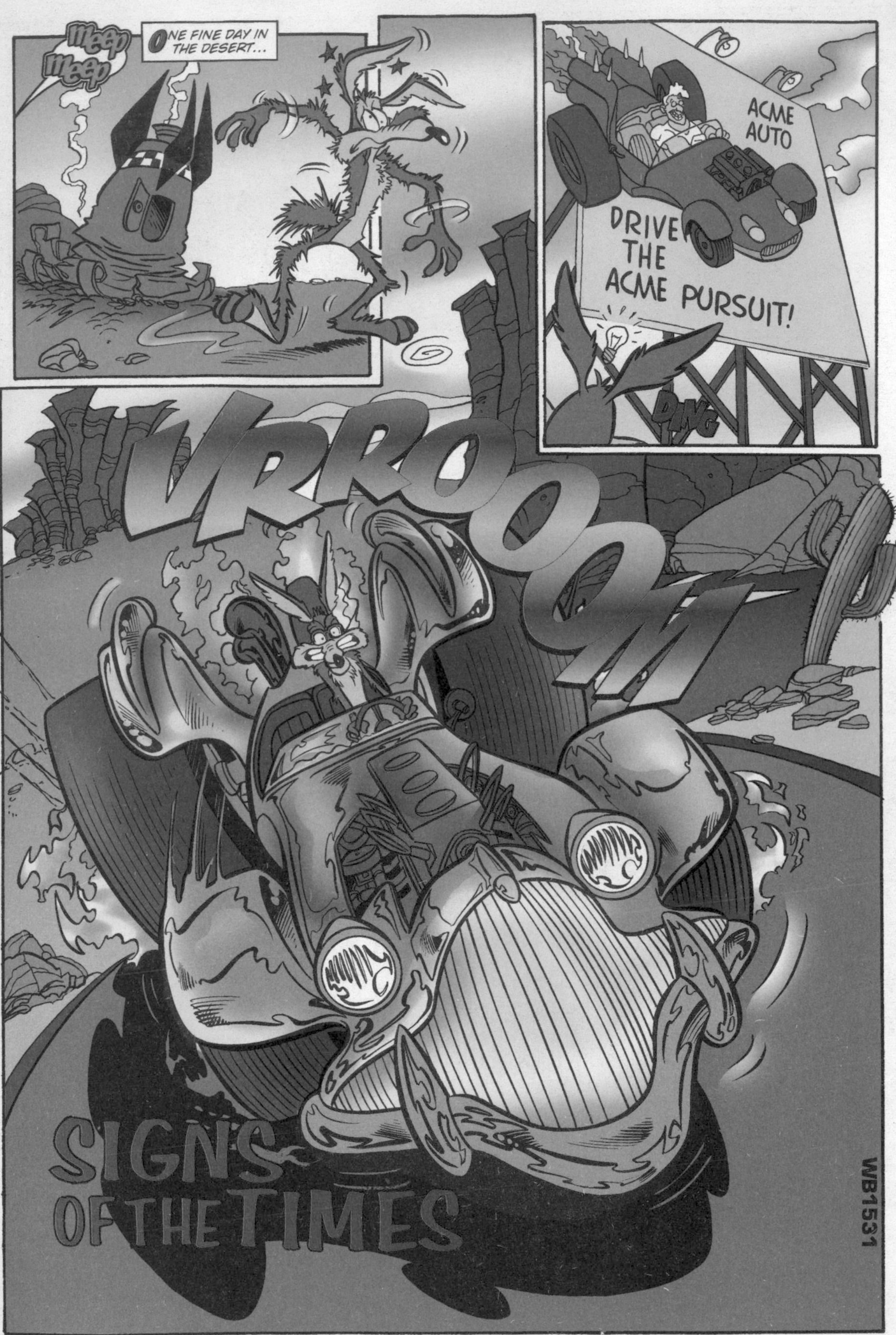

TERRY COLLINS WRITER • NELSON LUTY PENCILLER • HORACIO OTTOLINI INKS • COMICRAFT LETTERS • PRISMACOLOR COLORS

meep meep
VROOOOOOOM
AUTO HANDS ON.
CLIK
!
WHIRR
CLIK
!
CLAMP
CLAMP
WHOOSH
meep meep

VROOOM
AUTO HANDS ON.
OFF.
ON.
CLIK
CLIK
CLIK
TO DISENGAGE AUTO HANDS, PLEASE BRING VEHICLE TO A COMPLETE STOP.
SCREEE
FLING
THUNK
BUCKLE UP!
meep meep

meep meep
ACME SAFETY INFLATO-BAG
VROOM

AIRBAG WILL DEPLOY IN CASE OF SUDDEN STOP.

!
fweet!

FWUMP
ROAD RUNNER CROSSING
SCREE
meep meep

meep
meep
HSSSSS

HSSSSS

HSSSSS

POP

FLUMP

meep
meep
DING
ACME MEDICAL SUPPLIES
DRIVE THE ACME WHEELIE 5000!
meep
meep
VROOOM
THE END..?

Writer: David Cody Weiss Penciller: David Alvarez Inker: Mike DeCarlo Letterer: John Costanza Colors: Prismacolor

WISE QUACKER
HARE CLUB
WILL WORK FOR FOOD
AMATEUR COMEDY NIGHT $$ PRIZE
HEY, IT'S WORTH A SHOT.
GOOD EVENING, LADIES AND GERMS!

MY AGENT ARRANGED THIS GIG, SO I CAN'T BE A TOTAL FLOP--HE GETS TEN PERCENT OF THE BLAME!
TAP TAP

IN FACT MY AGENT JUST OPENED OFFICES ALL OVER THE WORLD.
SO NOW I'M UN-EMPLOYED IN 16 COUNTRIES!

HMM, TOUGH CROWD. OKAY...
TWO FLEAS WANTED TO GO TRAVELING...

BUT THEY COULDN'T DECIDE WHETHER TO WALK OR TO CATCH A DOG!

SILKWORMS MAKE THREAD, MOTHS MAKE HOLES.
I CROSSED ONE WITH THE OTHER AND GOT A BUG THAT MAKES LACE.

THEN I CROSSED A TERMITE WITH A PRAYING MANTIS.
NOW I HAVE A BUG THAT SAYS GRACE BEFORE IT EATS MY HOUSE!
BZZZZZZZZZZZZ

YAWN

ER... ACTUALLY, MY HOUSE IS IN SUCH BAD SHAPE THAT THE TERMITES EAT OUT.

IT'S A GREAT HOUSE, THOUGH--IT HAS HOT AND COLD RUNNING MICE.

Chirp...
chirp...
Chirp...

YOU'RE A NICE GROUP. WOULD YOU LIKE TO LEAVE A WAKE-UP CALL?!

HOW CAN YOU PEOPLE SLEEP WITH THESE LIGHTS ON?
I HOPE THE RED CROSS GETS HERE ON TIME. SHOULD I CALL 911?

HAH! MISSED ME!
THAT MAKES US EVEN--

--I MISSED YOUR LAUGHS!
BOO!
GO HOME!
YOU MUST BE A VEGETARIAN CROWD! EITHER THAT OR NOBODY HERE COULD AFFORD A STEAK TO POUND INTO MY HEART!

SPEAKING OF MEAT, WHY DON'T CANNIBALS EAT RABBIT STEW?
'CAUSE NOBODY WANTS A HARE IN THEIR SOUP!

HOW MANY RABBITS DOES IT TAKE TO MAKE A RUG?
ABOUT A DOZEN--IF YOU FLATTEN THEM OUT!

YIPE!
GRRR!

STAGE DOOR
SCRAM!
GET OUTTA HERE!

OH, WELL... IT'S A LIVING.
HARE CLUB
WILL JOKE FOR FOOD
That's All, Folks!

WB1520
WHATCHA DOIN', PUDDY?
NONE OF YOUR BUSINESS, BIRD-BOY! BUT IF YOU MUST KNOW...
...I'M PLANNING ON DOIN' SOME SKATIN'!
I NEVER SEEN WOLLER SKATES LIKE THOSE BEFORE!
THEY'RE CALLED ROLLERBLADES! ≈SHEESH≈ DON'T YOU EVER WATCH MTV?
GWACIOUS, NO! GWANNY SAYS WOCK VIDEOS WILL GIVE ME NIGHTMARES!
CRY "UNCLE!"
WRITER: TERRY COLLINS PENCILLER: PABLO ZAMBONI
INKER: RUBEN TORREIRO LETTERER: DANIEL GRIFFO
COLORIST: PRISMACOLOR

I AM GWAD TO SEE YOU GETTING EXERCISE, PUDDY!
NATCH! I'VE ALWAYS BEEN PHYSICALLY FIT! THERE'S ONLY ONE PROBLEM--

EXERCISIN' WORKS UP A CAT'S APPETITE!

I'M GOING DOWN TO THE MAILBOX, BOYS --BE GOOD WHILE I'M GONE!

YOU GONNA WEAD ME A STORY, PUDDY?
MAYBE LATER-- AFTER DINNER. 'SIDES, THESE BOOK AIN'T FOR READIN'!

OOH, GOODY! A WAMP! YOU GONNA DO SOME TWICKS?
UH-HUH! I'M GONNA TRY OUT MY DISAPPEARIN ACT -- YOU CAN BE MY PARTNER!

IF YOU'RE GONNA DO SKATE TWICKS, YOU'D BETTER WEAR PWOTECTION!

WHERE'S YOUR SAFETY HEWMET?

WEAR A HELMET INDOORS? GET REAL! HELMETS ARE FOR SISSIES AND AMATEURS!

SKRUNK!

WHICH ONE ARE YOU, PUDDY?

TWEETY! TWEETY! YOU GOT A LETTER!
THE RETURN ADDRESS SAYS IT CAME ALL THE WAY FROM WASHINGTON!

OH, THIS IS SO EXCITING! "DEAR TWEETY: THE TIME HAS COME FOR ME TO VISIT WITH MY FAVORITE NEPHEW."

"AS YOU KNOW, YOUR UNCLE SAMMY LIKES TO FLY AS CHEAPLY AS POSSIBLE..."
PHOOEY! I NEVER GET ANY MAIL!

"TO AVOID HIGH AIRLINE FARES AND THE STRESS OF A CROSS-COUNTRY FLIGHT, I HAVE DISCOVERED A NEW WAY TO TRAVEL."

HEH. THE OLD GUY MUST BE GETTING PRETTY LONG IN THE TOOTH.

MIGHT BE A BIT CHEWY, BUT I LIKE MY FOOD SEASONED!

"I WILL BE ARRIVING ON THE TENTH VIA OVERNIGHT MAIL. I FIND THIS TO BE THE CHEAPEST AND MOST RELIABLE METHOD FOR A BIRD ON A BUDGET.
"I NOW USE THEM FOR ALL MY JOURNEYS! AFTER ALL--I GET TO BRING MY BEDROOM WITH ME..., AND BAD WEATHER DOESN'T EVEN SLOW THE POST OFFICE DOWN!"

MY, ISN'T THAT INTERESTING -- A BIRD WHO TRAVELS BY POSTAL PACKAGE! YOU HAVE THE MOST CHARMING RELATIVES, TWEETY.

THE TENTH, EH? FIVE DAYS FROM NOW... MORE THAN ENOUGH TIME TO GET READY TO SAY "BON APPÉTIT" TO OUR GUEST!

FIVE DAYS LATER ...

ERT!

GAH! YOU STARTLED ME!

I GUESS YOU MUST REALLY BE EAGER FOR THIS OVERNIGHT PACKAGE!

HERE YOU GO, MA'AM!

ALL DONE!
OKAY, NOW I'LL--
HOLD IT! WAIT JUST
A MINUTE!

I CAN'T READ THIS!
I NEED A LEGIBLE SIGNATURE
BEFORE I CAN GIVE THIS
DELIVERY OVER TO--

--YOU? MA'AM?
WHERE'D YOU GO?
HMM. MAYBE
I'M AT THE WRONG
ADDRESS.

BETTER CHECK
THE PACKAGE AGAIN
AND --HEY!

GET OUTTA THERE!
DON'T YOU KNOW IT'S A
FEDERAL OFFENSE TO
TAMPER WITH THE MAIL?

A KITTY CAT IN OLD LADY DRAG. MY THERAPIST WILL HAVE A FIELD DAY WITH THIS!
STILL, MAIL TAMPERING IS MAIL TAMPERING...
♫

WHOA!
SPROING!

STEADY! STEADY! A MAIL CARRIER ALWAYS KEEPS HIS FOOTING!

BAD FOR THE OL' IMAGE IF HE TRIPS AND FALLS DOWN ON THE JOB!
YEE-OWW!

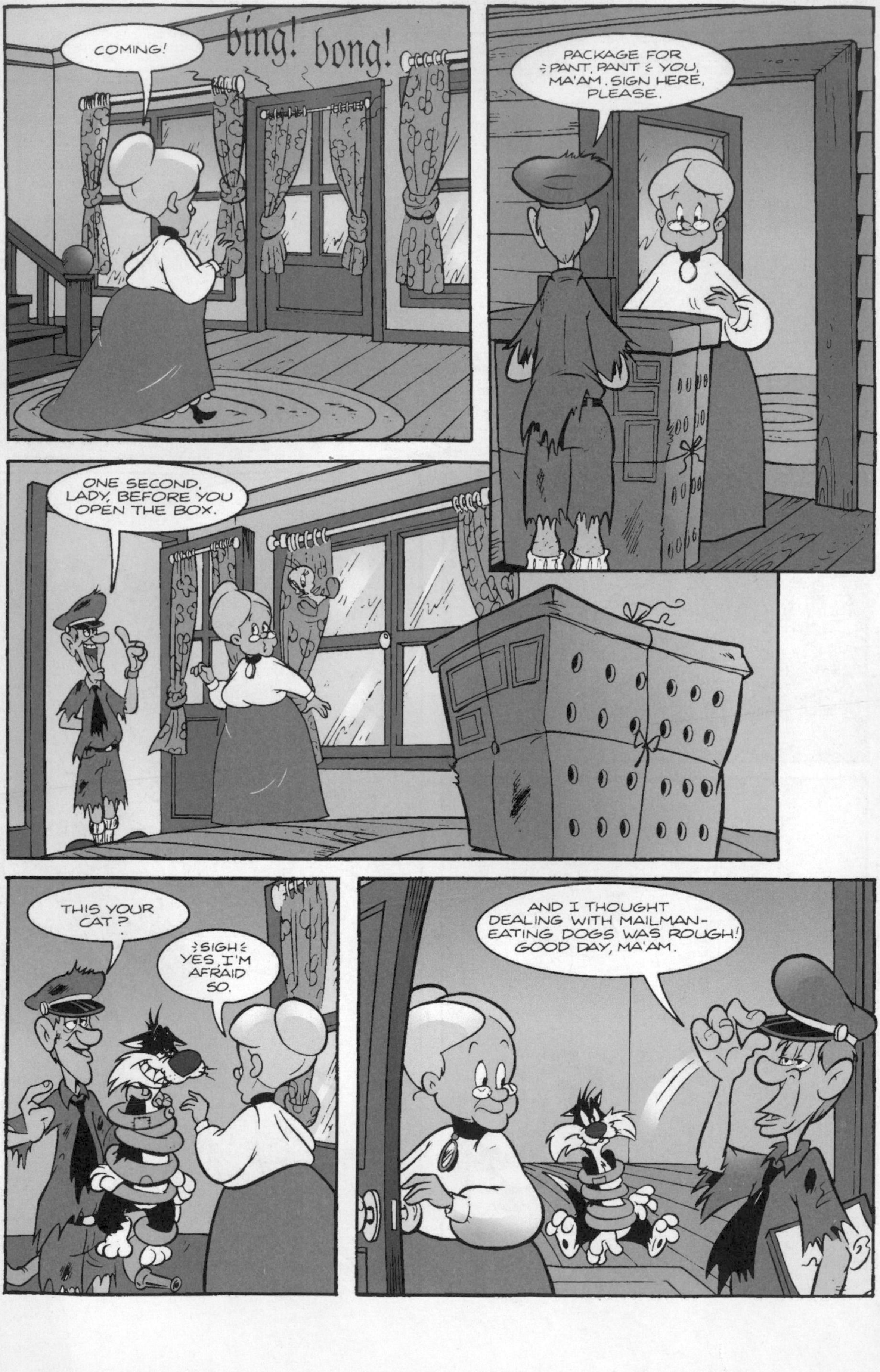

COMING!

bing! bong!

PACKAGE FOR ≷PANT, PANT≷ YOU, MA'AM. SIGN HERE, PLEASE.

ONE SECOND, LADY, BEFORE YOU OPEN THE BOX.

BAD KITTY! YOU SHOULD BE ASHAMED--WE HAVE COMPANY IN THE HOUSE!
NOW BEHAVE YOURSELF WHILE I FETCH MY SCISSORS!
WHY WAIT? I GOT MY OWN PAIR RIGHT HERE!
SPROING!
MY, BUT YOU'RE BEING HELPFUL, PUDDY.
THINK NOTHIN' OF IT. ALWAYS GLAD TO WELCOME ANOTHER BIRDIE TO THE MENU!
YOU CAME A LONG WAY TO BE A ... BOXED ...
GULP ... LUNCH?
AH, FEELS GOOD TO STRETCH MY WINGS AFTER BEING COOPED UP IN THERE!
HIYA, KID.
HEWWO, UNCLE SAMMY!

YOU MUST BE THE CAT I HEARD SO MUCH ABOUT.
I *HATE* CATS.
OOOO! YOU'RE WUCKY, PUDDY! UNCLE SAMMY IS GIVING YOU A KICKBOXING WESSON!
HOW DID YOU KNOW THAT BACK HOME HE WAS CHAMP TEN YEARS WUNNING?

ONE PAINFUL VISIT FROM UNCLE SAMMY LATER...
HEY, MISTER LITTLETON-- THIS IS A NEW ONE! GOT A GUY WHO WANTS TO KNOW IF WE TAKE CATS!
SURE BUDDY, WE DELIVER CATS. WE'RE THE POST OFFICE--WE'LL SHIP ANYTHING!
SCHEDULE A PICK-UP? YOU BET!
WHATCHA DOIN', PUDDY?
WHAT'S IT LOOK LIKE? I'M SHIPPING MYSELF TO ANTARCTICA.
DOWN THERE, TH'ONLY BIRDS I GOTTA DEAL WITH ARE *PENGUINS!*
AN*ARTICA
That's All, Folks!

Writer: Dan Slott Penciller: David Alvarez Inker: Mike DeCarlo Letterer: John Costanza Colorist: David Tanguay

GO, MY FAITHFUL MINION! FIND ME MORE BRAINS! BRAINS!
AWW, GO GET 'EM YOURSTHELF! WHAT DO I LOOK LIKE? YOUR MAID?
VERY WELL--I'LL JUST HAVE TO USE--YOURS!
MWAH HA HA!
THSURE THING, BOSSTH! AND HOW WOULD YOU LIKE YOUR BRAINSTH?
OVER EASTHY? THSUNNY THSIDE UP? I AIM TO PLEASTHE!

AWWW, WHERE AM I GONNA FIND A BRAIN AT THIS HOUR? AND IN THIS NEIGHBORHOOD, NO LESSTH?!
OH WOOK, A PUDDY-TAT!

HEWWO, MR. PUDDY-TAT! WATCHA DOIN'?
AH THSCRAM! I DON'T HAVE TIME FOR THISTH! I GOTTA FIND SOME BRAINSTH!

MAYBE I COULD HELP!
NOW WET ME THINK... HMM... BWAINS...

HEY! WHAT'RE YOU WOOKING AT?!
GRADE A

OOOH! HEWP! SOMEBODY HEWP ME! THE BAD OL' PUDDY'S GOT ME!
AH HA! I GOTSTH YOU NOW! YOU AND YOUR LITTLE BRAIN!

WEALLY? YOU WANT ME FOR MY BWAIN?
NORMAWWY I'D FIGHT... BUT PART OF ME IS SO FWATTERED!

MWAH HA HA! THROW THE SWITCH!
YESTH MASTHTER!
ZZAP!

JUMPIN' G. HOSSTHEPHAT!
IT'S ALIVE! ALIVE! IT'S...

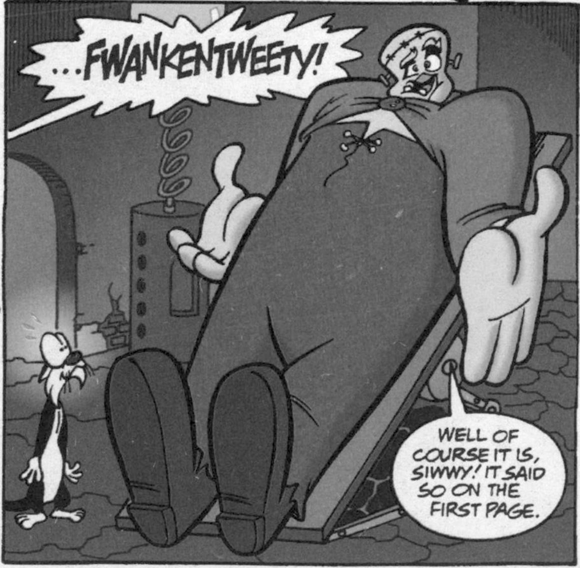
...FWANKENTWEETY!
WELL OF COURSE IT IS, SIWWY! IT SAID SO ON THE FIRST PAGE.

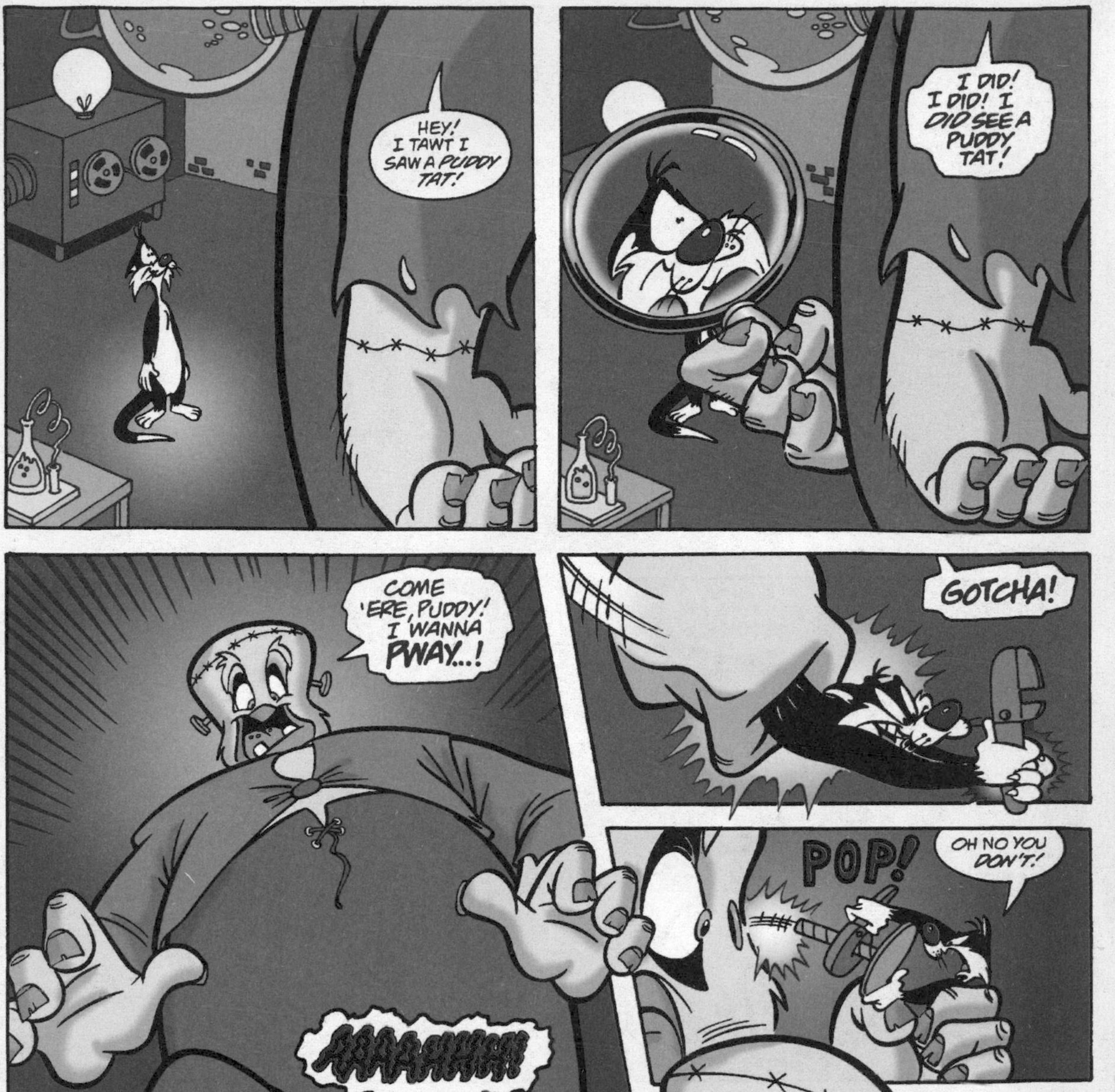

COME 'ERE, PUDDY! I WANNA PWAY...!

AAAAHHHH!

GOTCHA!

POP!

OH NO YOU DON'T!

OOH, YOU BAD OL PUDDY TAT!

YOU'RE GONNA BE IN SO MUCH TWOUBLE WHEN I GET MY BIG OL' HEAD BACK ON!

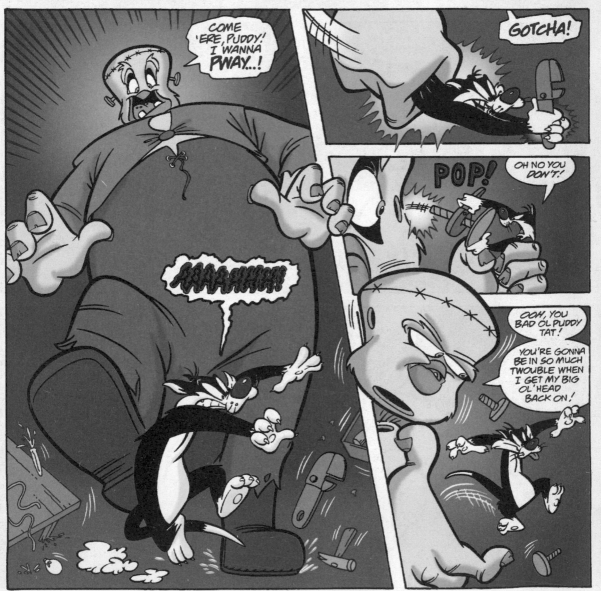

OH PUDDY... WHERE AWE YOU?...
COME OUT, COME OUT WHERE EVVAH YOU AWE! OH, IT'S MUCH TOO DAWK IN HERE!

I KNOW! I'LL TURN ON THE WIGHTS!
ZZZZAP!

OOPS! WAS I BAD?

HE'S COMING TO!
THE EXPERIMENT IS A SUCCESS! IT WORKED--

--IT'S ALIVE!
HEY! WHAT'STH GOIN' ON?
BEHOLD, I HAVE MADE YOU...
THE BWIDE OF FWANKENTWEETY!
OOOH! DON'T YOU WOOK WAVISHING!
EEEEE!
OH NO YOU DON'T, BUSTHTER!
PUDDY! COME BACK!
AW WELL! AT WEAST HE TOOK MY HAND IN MATWIMONY!
That's ARM, Folks!

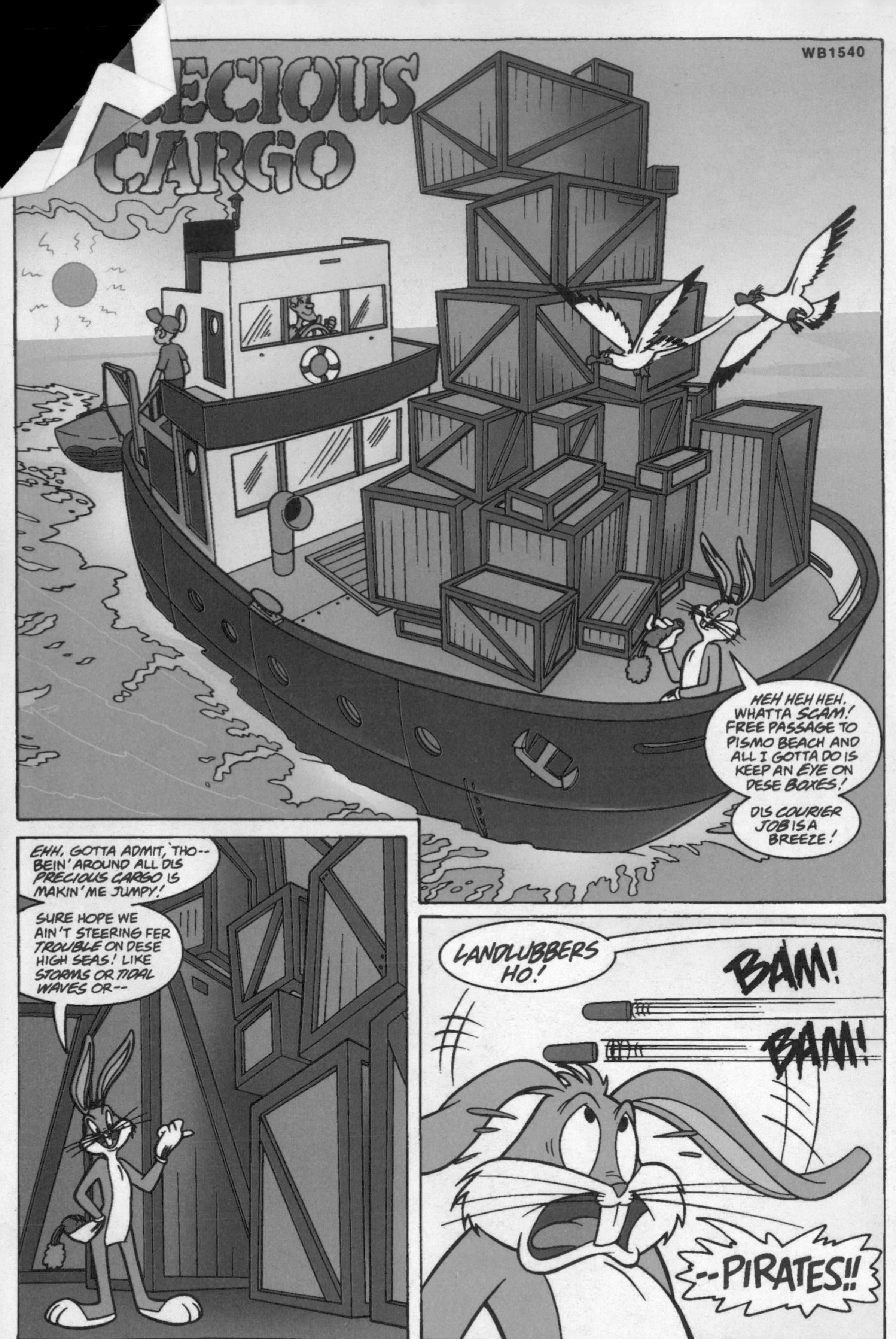

Writer: Terry Collins Penciller: Nelson Luty Inker: Jim Amash Letterer: John Costanza Colorist: Prismacolor

EH, FOR A LITTLE GUY HE'S GOTTA PRETTY BIG MOUTH!
AH'MA YOSEMITE SAM, AND AH'MA TAKIN' OVER THIS SHIP!
SO DON'T GET ANY FUNNY IDEAS--THAR'S PLENTY MORE BULLETS WHAR THOSE CAME FROM!

NOW THAT AH GOTS YER ATTENTION, LET ME TELL YUH ABOUT MUHSELF!
AH'M THE ROUGHEST, TOUGHEST SEA DOG TO EVER THROW A DOGFISH A BONE, FLOAT A BOAT, OR KEEL-HAUL A SCURVY KNAVE!

AH'M THE SCOURGE OF THE SEVEN SEAS AND AH STOMP IN EVERY MUD PUDDLE AH MEET!
AH'MA SO MEAN OTHER PIRATES TAKE UP GARDENING WHEN THEY SEE ME--
EHHH, EXCUSE ME, DOC...

WHADDAYA YOU WANT, RABBIT?!
ARE YOU SURE YOU'RE A PIRATE? I SEEN BETTER PIRATES IN TH' BATHTUB.

WHY YOU-- YOU--
OOOOOH!!

THEM'S FIGHTIN' WORDS, YOU MANGY LOP-EARED CRITTER!
JEST ASKIN', DOC.
WULL, LOOK AT MAH SHIP-- "THE BLOODY MAST!" ONLY PIRATES HAVE SHIPS LIKE THAT!
THAT PLEASURE CRUISER? I BET YOU RENTED THAT ALONG WITH YOUR CUTE LI'L PIRATE COSTUME.
I'M NOT WEARING ANY COSTUME, YOU FLOP-EARED GALOOT!!
WHAT DO YOU THINK A PIRATE LOOKS LIKE?
WELL, HE HAS A WOODEN LEG, A HOOK FOR A HAND, A CUTLASS, A PARROT, A PATCH OVER ONE EYE, A SPOTTED BANDANNA...
RABBIT'S GOT A POINT.
YEAH, WHERE'S YOUR PARROT?
WHY AH--AH-- YOU DAD-BLASTED--

OOOOOOOH!
I'LL SHOW YOU WHO'S A PIRATE!!!

I'LL **PROVE** TO YUH AH'MA **PIRATE!**
HOW YA GONNA DO *THAT,* DOC?

AH'MA GONNA MAKE YUH **WALK THE PLANK!**
WELL, SHIVER ME TIMBERS--A DIVING BOARD!

MUSTN'T GET MY EARS WET!
HURRY UP AND **JUMP!**

OOOOOOH, I HOPE THE WATER AIN'T TOO *COLD!*
JUMP! 'FORE I HAVE TO GO AND **BLAST** YUH!
SPROING SPROING

SPLASH
THAT'LL SHOW THAT GALOOT AH'MA *PIRATE!* NOW TO GO LOOTIN' AND PLUNDERIN'!

OOOH, IT WAS TOO COLD!
EHHHH, SO WHATCHA DOIN' NOW, DOC?
WHAT DOES IT LOOK LIKE? AH'M OPENIN' THIS HERE BOX!

YA DON'T SAY. WHADDAYA DOIN' THAT FOR?
LOOT! THIS TUB IS LOADED TO THE GILLS WITH PRECIOUS CARGO!

PRECIOUS CARGO, EH? WHAT KINDA PRECIOUS CARGO?
AH'M NOT RIGHTLY SURE, BUT IT COULD BE--
DIAMONDS!

DIAMONDS?!
SHHH! NOT SO LOUD! YOU WANT EVERYBODY TO HEAR?!

OOOH, DIAMONDS!
DIAMONDS!
DIAMONDS!
DIS I GOTTA SEE FOR MYSELF! CAN I HELP? CAN I DOC, CAN I, CAN I, HUH???
YES YES YES, ANYTHING, JEST HUSH UP!

YOU GOT IT, DOC! FIRST BOX, COMIN' THROUGH!
THUNK!
HEADS UP!
WHAM!
NO DIAMONDS YET? TRY DIS ONE!
WATCH IT, RABBIT!
CHEE, YOU PIRATE TYPES SURE ARE CLUMSY!
CLONGGG

WAAAH! WAAAAAH! I WANT MUH DIAMONDS! WAAAH!
OH, BRUDDER.

COME ON, COME ON, QUIT CRYIN'; YA BIG TOUGH PIRATE. IF I SHOW YA THE PRECIOUS CARGO, WILL YA QUIT BLUBBERIN'?
IF I GIVE IT TO YA, YA GOTTA PROMISE TA GO AND NOT COME BACK!
Y-Y-YEAH.
AH PROMISE.

MEBBE YUH AREN'T SO BAD AFTER ALL, RABBIT!
READY...?

CATCH!

NOW WHERE DID THE LITTLE GUY GO?

MINE, MINE, ALL MINE!
AH CLAIM THIS PRECIOUS CARGO IN THE NAME OF YOSEMITE SAM!

BON VOY-AGEE, PIRATE BOY! REMEMBER TA KEEP BOTH OARS IN THE WATER!

MINE MINE MINE MINE MINE!
AH CAIN'T A-HARDLY WAIT TUH SEE IT! GOLD, SAPPHIRES, DIAMONDS--

SMOOOSH

--CARROTS?!!?
HEH HEH HEH! WELL, THEY ARE PRECIOUS CARGO...
...TO A RABBIT!
That's All, Folks!

Writer: Michael Eury Penciller: Oscar Saavedra Inker: Ruben Torreiro Letterer: Javier Saavedra Colorist: Dave Tanguay

HURRY UP, BOY, BEFORE SOME **WEASEL** COMES ALONG AN' EATS IT!

ACME

DAWG

HA-HA!

URRRK!

TWANGG

DAW

HENERY HAWK
WILL DEVOUR ANY CHICKEN, NO MATTER THE SIZE.
HENERY@LOONEY.COM
NAW- LIKE I NEED ANOTHER BIRDBRAIN AROUND HERE?
TASMANIAN DEVIL
VORACIOUS APPETITE. FOND OF RABBIT (AND CHICKEN) MEAT.
TAZ@LOONEY.COM
NOW HERE'S DA GUY FOR DA JOB! A BIG WOOLLY MAMMAL, LIKE ME!
I'LL JEST INVITE THIS TASMANIAN OVER FOR A NICE FRIED CHICKEN DINNER.
IT'S THE SOUTHERN WAY!
TAK TAK
WHOOOSSH
I WONDER HOW LONG HE'LL TAKE TA ANSWER MY MESSA--
WHOOSH
YEOWWW!

MOOOooo!
SHOOOOOOSH!
WHAT THE SAM HILL???
CHICKEN$#@*!
PERHAPS AH HAVE BITTEN OFF MORE THAN AH CAN CHEW HERE...
WHAT, AH SAY, WHAT'S ALL THIS RUCKUS ABOUT, SON?
CHICKEN$#@*!
"CONGRATULATIONS! YOU HAVE WON A SPECIAL "FATHEADED FRIED CHICKEN" MEAL. YOU MUST APPEAR IN PERSON TO CLAIM YOUR PRIZE!"
"FATHEADED CHICKEN?!" AH SAY, WHY, AH SAY THERE'S NO SUCH THING!
SURE THERE IS. JEST LOOK AT THAT BIG FAT HEAD! YOUR CHOLESTE-ROL MUST GO UP JEST LOOKIN' THE MIRROR!
*%$!! FATHEAD YUM! *%#!!
NOW WAIT JEST A MINUTE HERE, SON...

ONE CHICKEN DINNER--TO GO!
OOF!!
#$&.!!CHICKEN#+!!
HOLD ON, BOY--
--WE CAN'T TALK IF YOUR MOUTH'S FULL!
MUNCHH!

%$%!! TAZ WANT FRIED CHICKEN!
FRIED CHICKEN? WELL, TAKE A GOOD LOOK AT ME, BOY!
AH AIN'T FRIED! NOT EVEN PLUCKED YET! THAT DAWG'S BEEN DOIN' SOME FALSE ADVERTISIN'.
I'D TAKE IT UP WITH HIM, IF I WAS YOU. RUN ALONG NOW, IT'S MY NAPTIME.
ASK ME, THAT BOY'S BRAIN IS BARBECUED, PULLIN' A STUNT LIKE THIS.
$#$!! BARBEQUE...?
SNIFF! SNIFF!
KOFF KOFF! WHAT THE--
YOU AGAIN!! Y'ALL DON'T GIVE UP, DO YA, BOY?
$#$#YUM!*&!!
YEOWWCH! MY TAIL FEATHERS!! AH'M PLUMB BURNT TO A CRISP!
MMM #&*! CRISPY!

SHOOP
OOOF!
WHUMP

WHOA, I SAY!
WHOA!

OOOOOOOOOOH!

$#$$! BARBEQUED CHICKEN **BURRITO** -- TAZ LIKE! *$#@!!!

BLUMP

SLOW DOWN, BOY! YOU DONE TRIED TO EAT ME RAW, BAKED, BBQ, AND TEX-MEX -- WHAT DO Y'ALL THINK AH AM, A ONE-ROOSTER **SMÖRGASBORD**?

AH THOUGHT IT WAS **FRIED** CHICKEN Y'ALL WANTED.

&*%$!! **FRIED** CHICKEN. YEAH, YEAH!

THEN Y'ALL GOT IT ALL WRONG, SON. SAYS HERE IN THE "SOUTHERN FRIED COOKBOOK" FRIED CHICKEN'S GOTTA BE DIPPED IN BOILIN' OIL.
NOW, I DON'T SEE ANY BOILING OIL AROUND HERE, DO YOU? THIS HERE IS A FARM, NOT A FAST-FOOD RESTAURANT.
TAZ NO WANT OILY BOIL. TAZ WANT FRIED CHICKEN!

YOU AIN'T QUITE COOKIN' WITH A FULL RECIPE, ARE YA, BOY?
IF Y'ALL GOT A COMPLAINT ABOUT BEIN' PROMISED FRIED CHICKEN, THEN TAKE IT UP WITH TH' PROMISER HERE.
GULP!
TAZ WANT CHICKEN!!!

WHY TAZ NOT EAT YET??!
WHY, I'VE BEEN SETTIN' UP THE OIL! OUT HERE WE LET THE GUESTS FOR THEIR OWN CHICKEN-- IT'S THE SOUTHERN WAY!
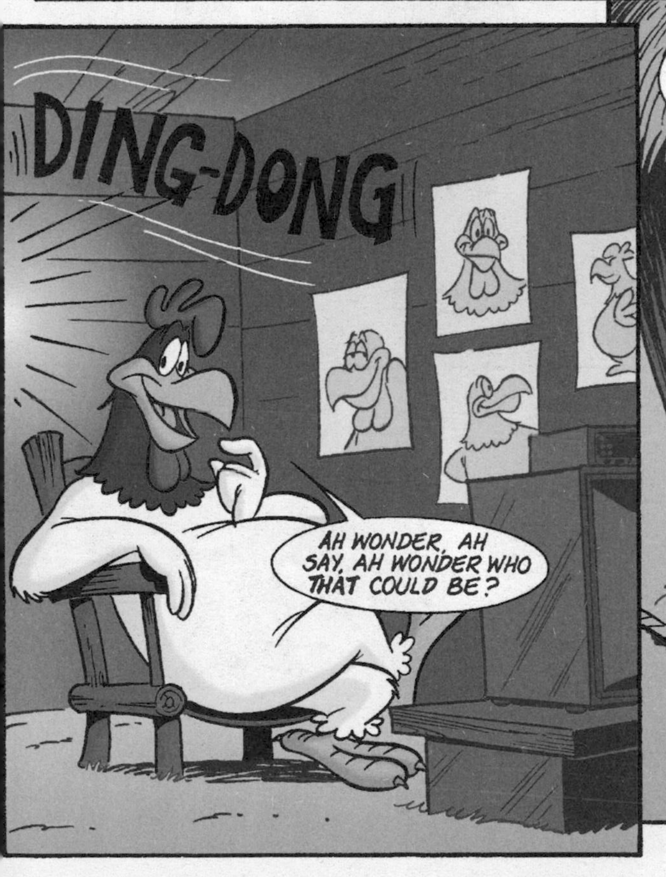
DING-DONG
AH WONDER, AH SAY, AH WONDER WHO THAT COULD BE?

NOBODY'S HERE. MUST BE A PRACTICAL JOKE PLAYED BY ONE 'A THEM JUVENILE DELINQUENTS...
WHAT, AH SAY WHAT IS WRONG WITH OUR YOUNG PEOPLE THESE DAYS?

FWIP
YOW!!
&*$#!!! TAZ FRY HIS OWN CHICKEN!
LOOKS LIKE THERE'S A COOKOUT GOIN' ON-AN' AH'M TH' MAIN COURSE!
NOW LOOKEE HERE, SON.. YOU DON'T WANT TO EAT ME. AIN'T YOU HEARD THAT FRIED CHICKEN'S LOADED WITH CHOLESTEROL?
WHAT THAT?
BAD STUFF, SON! IT MAKES YA FAT-- CLOGS YOUR ARTERIES!
TAZ FAT? TAZ CLOGGED?
BUT TAZ HUNGRY!
WELL, LEMME TELL YA WHAT IS GOOD TO EAT THEN, SON...
FISH!
%$&!! FISH!! WHERE TAZ GET FISH?!
Y'ALL'S IN LUCK, BOY. THERE'S ONE KIND OF FISH THAT LIVES ON THIS HERE FARM..

--THE DAWGFISH! AN' AH SEE ONE RIGHT OVER YONDER!

AWK!

DOGFISH! YUM YUM! $%#!!!

ENJOY! BONE APPETIT!

"BONE" APPETIT.. GET IT? THAT'S A JOKE, SON. HA HA!

$%#@!!!!

END

A PIZZA MY MIND

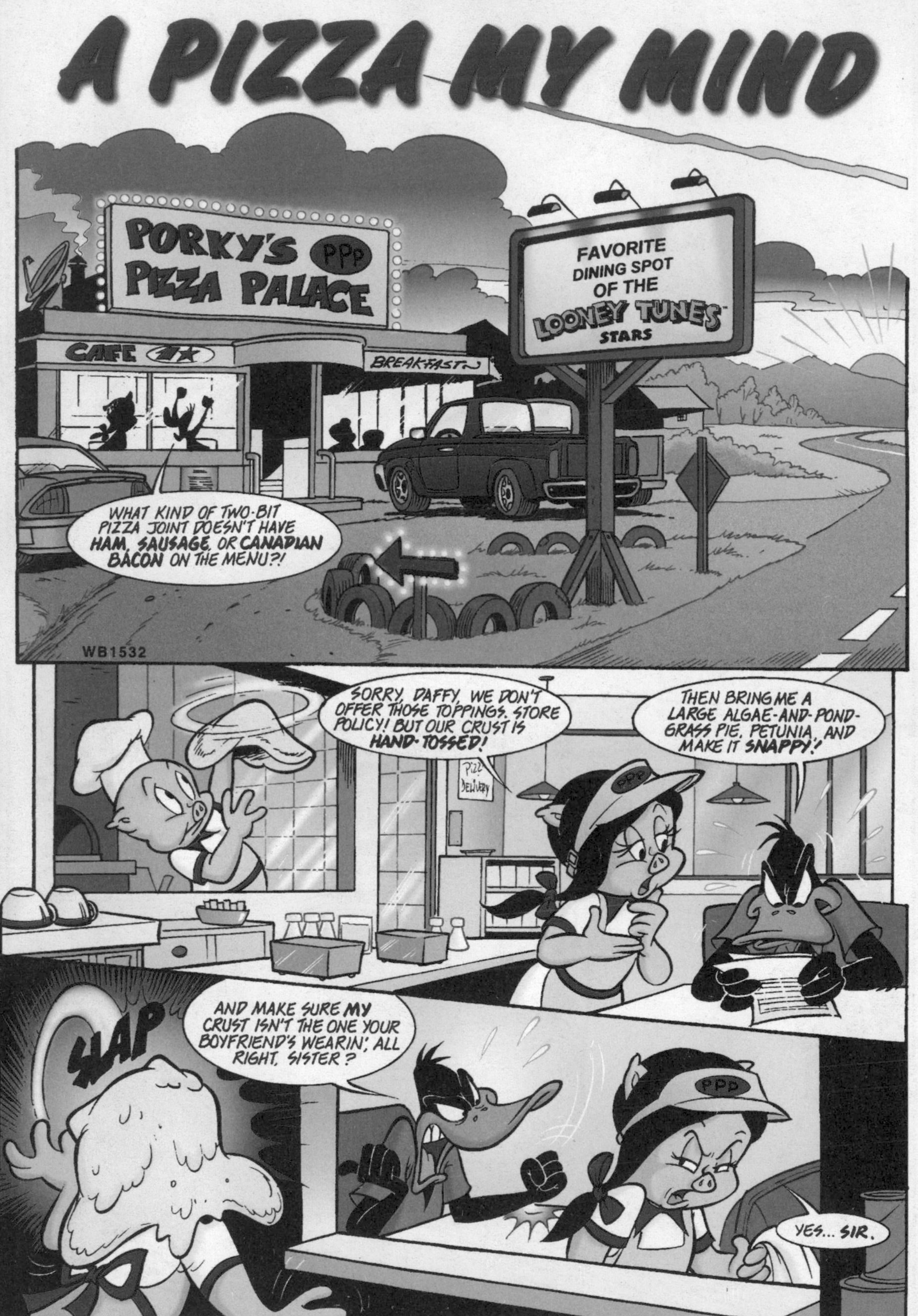

Writer: Michael Eury Penciller: Horacio Saavedra Inker: Ruben Torreiro Letterer: Javier Saavedra Colorist: David Tanguay

LOONEY TUNES PHOTO GALLERY.
WAAAIT A MINUTE... SOMEONE'S MISSING!
HEY, PORKSTER--YOU'VE EVEN GOT THE LOONEY TUNES PROPS UP HERE! SO HOW COME THERE'S NO PICTURE OF ME ON THE WALL ??!
BUGS BUNNY
A-A-ACTUALLY, DAFFY, THERE'S--
THERE'S SOMETHIN' ROTTEN HERE, AND IT AIN'T YOUR LIMBURGER AND GARLIC PIZZA!
IT'S THE SMELL OF DUCK DISCRIMINATION!
OF COURSE NOT, DAFFY. THE REASON YOUR P-P-PICTURE ISN'T HERE IS--
--IS THAT YOU DON'T HAVE AN APPROPRIATE SHOT THAT TRULY CAPTURES MY UNPAR-ALLELED HANDSOMENESS! RIGHT?!
THEN SAY NO MORE, PORKY--I'LL SEE THAT YOU GET ONE.

TAZ, OL' BUDDY, I NEED A **FAVOR**.
>MUNCH MUNCH MUNCH< **HMM**?
I'VE GOTTA HAVE A SNAPSHOT TAKEN, SO **HERE**--TAKE A **SNAP**.
TAZ TAKE **SNACK**?!?

TAZ LIKE SNACK! >**GULP**!<
HEY! MY CAMERA!
CLICK
URP!!
WHAT A **DIMBULB**! NOW I'LL HAVE TO FIND **ANOTHER** WAY TO GET MY PICTURE MADE.

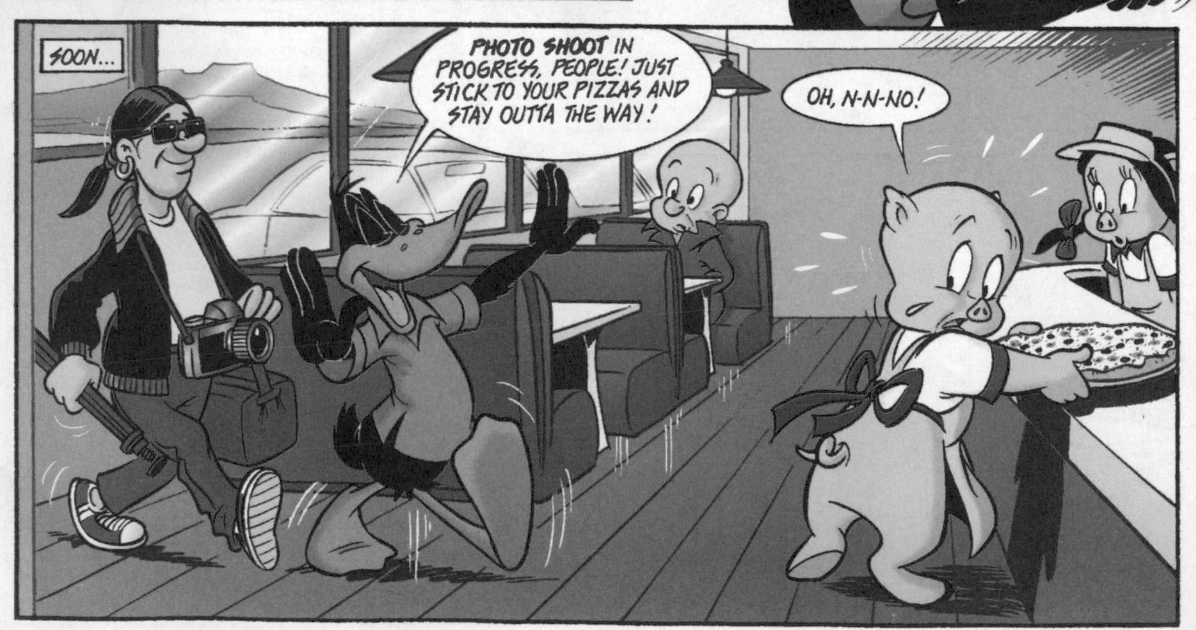
SOON...
PHOTO SHOOT IN PROGRESS, PEOPLE! JUST STICK TO YOUR PIZZAS AND STAY OUTTA THE WAY!
OH, N-N-NO!

PORKY, I FORGIVE YOU FOR YOUR CARELESS OVERSIGHT OF OMITTING ME FROM YOUR PHOTO GALLERY.
AND TO SHOW YOU WHAT A GOOD SPORT I AM, YOU'LL SOON HAVE AN ENTIRE WALL OF PICTURES OF YOURS TRULY.
D-DAFFY, YOU'VE GOT IT ALL WR- WR- WRONG...
AWAY, PORKY. YOU'RE BLOCKING MY LIGHT.
YOU CAN'T TREAT ME LIKE THIS! I'M THE PROPRI-- PROPRI-- THE BOSS!
LIKE I CARE. BEGONE! I MUST BEGIN MY WORK!
YES, DAFFY, YES! THE CAMERA LOVES YOU!!!

THAT DAFFY DUCK IS GONNA RU--RU--RU--MESS UP MY BUSINESS!
UH-OH
SLAP
HEY--!
WHO DARES?!
WHY DOESN'T ANYONE HERE RESPECT MY ARTISTIC GENIUS?!!
UH, I'LL JUST EAT AT THE WESTAUWANT DOWN THE WOAD.
I CANNOT WORK IN THESE DEPLORABLE CONDITIONS!!
MARK MY WORDS, BUSTER-- ONE WAY OR ANOTHER, MY PHOTO WILL BE ON YOUR WALL!
AWWW, GET OUT AND STAY OUT, YOU SC- SC- SCREWY DUCK!

LATER...
THANKS TO THAT STUPID PIG'S MEDDLING, I'M FORCED TO SNEAK IN MY PHOTO.
DO NOT OBSTRUCT
UGH! MY PICTURE! IT'S STUCK... WON'T BUDGE...
DARN TH-THAT SILLY DUCK! HE'S KEPT ME SO D-D-DISTRACTED, I LET MY OVEN GET COLD.
WOO! WOO! WOO-HOO HOO!
YIKES!!
FWOOSH
HOTT
HOT
HOTTT!
THAT PIG IS REALLY STARTING TO BURN ME UP!

SHORTLY...
WHUP WHUP WHUP
WHAT'S THAT?
SEE, PORKY? I PROMISED YOU A PICTURE!
PALACE
PPP
Breakfast
SNAP!
CRASH
BBOOM

YOU DE--DE--WRECKED MY RESTAURANT, YOU CRAZY DUCK!
WELL, IT NEVER WOULDA HAPPENED IF YOU'D PUT MY PICTURE ON YOUR WALL IN THE FIRST PLACE.
MR. PIG?
I PUT THIS PICTURE IN A BRAND-NEW FRAME. LIKE YOU ASKED.
ACME FRAMING SHOP
TH-TH-THAT'S WHAT I'VE BEEN TRYING TO TELL YOU, DAFFY. YOUR PICTURE WAS BEING RE-FRA-FRA-FRAMED.
OH, SILLY ME.

HOW COME IT'S NOT DIAMOND-STUDDED?
OH, B-B-BROTHER.
SEVERAL MONTHS LATER...
PORKY PIG'S NEW PIZZA PALACE
-GRAND RE-OPENING-
EVEN THOUGH THAT PESKY DUCK IS IN J-JAIL--

--I'M GLAD I STILL HAVE HIS P-P-PICTURE IN MY RESTAURANT!
The End

Writer: Michael Eury Penciller: Pablo Zamboni Inker: Ruben Torreiro Letterer: John Costanza Colors: Prismacolor

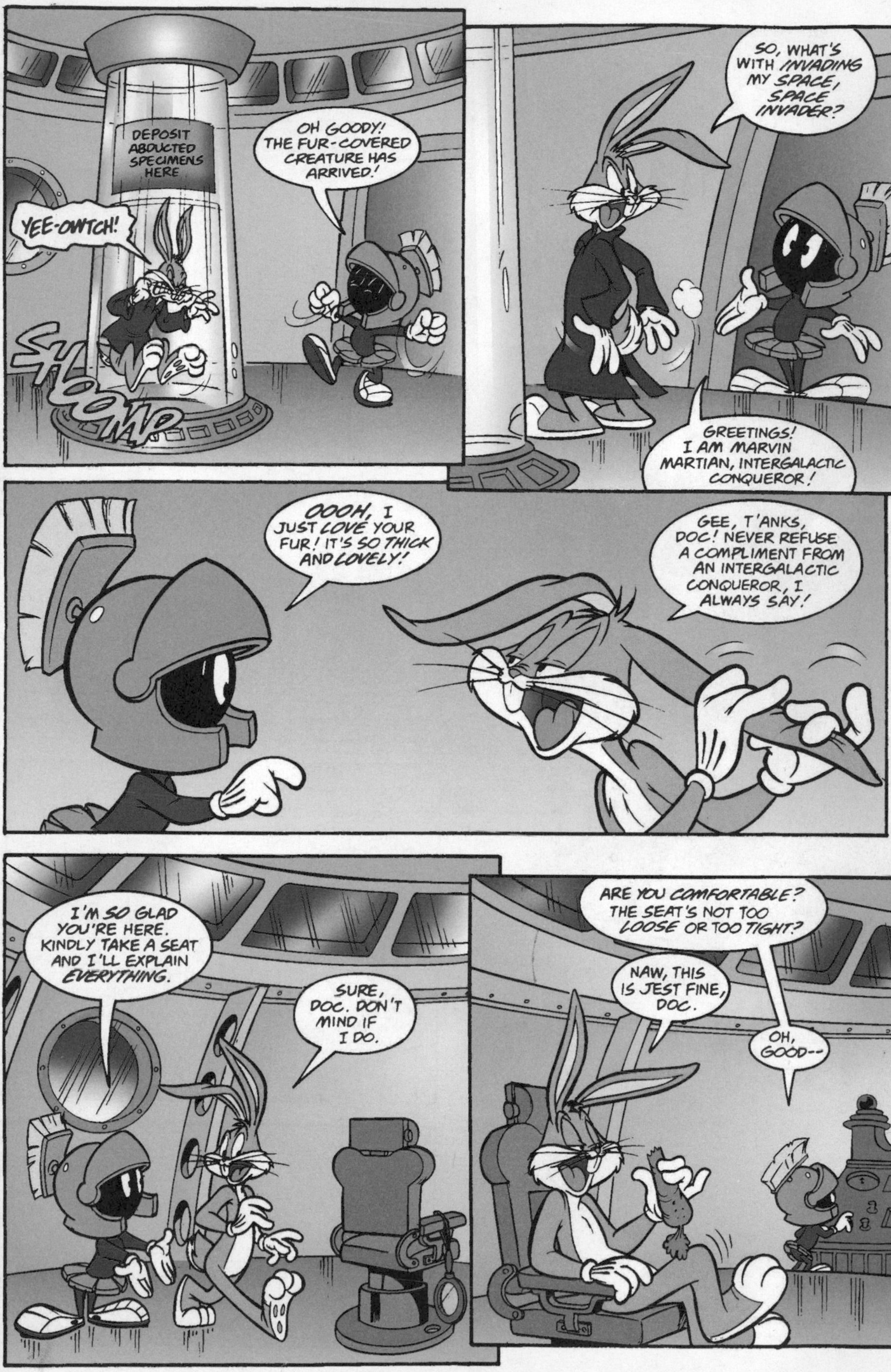

DEPOSIT ABDUCTED SPECIMENS HERE
OH GOODY! THE FUR-COVERED CREATURE HAS ARRIVED!
YEE-OWTCH!
SHLOOMP
SO, WHAT'S WITH INVADING MY SPACE, SPACE INVADER?
GREETINGS! I AM MARVIN MARTIAN, INTERGALACTIC CONQUEROR!
OOOH, I JUST LOVE YOUR FUR! IT'S SO THICK AND LOVELY!
GEE, T'ANKS, DOC! NEVER REFUSE A COMPLIMENT FROM AN INTERGALACTIC CONQUEROR, I ALWAYS SAY!
I'M SO GLAD YOU'RE HERE. KINDLY TAKE A SEAT AND I'LL EXPLAIN EVERYTHING.
SURE, DOC. DON'T MIND IF I DO.
ARE YOU COMFORTABLE? THE SEAT'S NOT TOO LOOSE OR TOO TIGHT?
NAW, THIS IS JEST FINE, DOC.
OH, GOOD--

HARE REMOVER
THIS IS NUTS! LEMME OUTTA HERE!
I'M AFRAID I CANNOT DO THAT, FURRY EARTH BEING. YOU SEE, SPACE IS DREADFULLY COLD. I NEED YOUR HAIR TO KEEP ME WARM AS I CONQUER THE GALAXY.
IT'S QUITE AN HONOR. AND IT WON'T HURT A BIT.
IT WON'T?
OH NO, THE PROCESS ITSELF IS PERFECTLY HARMLESS...
...PITY ABOUT THOSE NASTY SIDE EFFECTS.
SIDE EFFECTS...?
ISN'T TECHNOLOGY DELIGHTFUL?
--THE X-3924 FOLLICULAR MODULATOR WON'T WORK PROPERLY IF YOU SQUIRM.
YIPE!

BZZAP

KZZZZZAP

OH MY!

OOOO, THAT EARTH CREATURE HAS MADE ME VERY ANGRY!

HEH-HEH! NOW THAT NAPOLEON'S NAPPIN', I'M GETTIN' OUTTA HERE!
WHERE ARE YOU, HAIRY EARTH CREATURE?
YEEP!

COME OUT! OR I'LL BE VERY CRANKY!

OH, SWEETIE DARLING, THERE YOU ARE! I'VE BEEN LOOKING FOR YOU JUST EVERY-WHERE!
...YOU HAVE?
HEAVENS, JUST LOOK AT YOU! TSK TSK! WHERE TO BEGIN?

SPACE CENTRAL SENT ME RIGHT OVER. NOW JUST LEAVE THIS TO ME. I'M NOT JUST THE PRESIDENT OF THE HARE CLUB FOR MARTIANS--

--I'M ALSO A MEMBER!
OOOOH, HOW LOVELY!

HEH-HEH! THINK THAT'S BAD, BRUDDER, I'M JUST GETTIN' STARTED!

NOW DON'T YOU MOVE A MUSCLE. MUSTN'T MUSS THE HAIR, MUST WE, DARLING?
OH NO, NATURALLY NOT!

HERE'S A LITTLE POINTER ALL THE GOILS BACK HOME TAWK ABOUT!
A LITTLE DAB'LL DO YA!
SPACE
ACME
CONCRETE

♪ I DREAM OF JEANNIE with the light BROW-OWN HAIR... ♫
BLOOSH
ACME

TOK
TOK
HEH HEH HEH. DON'T LET THE BOYS TAKE YOU FOR GRANITE, DOC!

WHATTA MAROON!
NOW TO SCRAM THIS FLYING SARDINE CAN--

GLEEP!
EXCUSE ME, MADAME PRESIDENT, BUT THIS IS TERRIBLY STIFF.

TAKES ONE TO KNOW ONE, DARLING -- BUT YOU'RE THE BOSS! I KNEW A GAL USED TOO MUCH OF THIS STUFF AND HER HAIR FELL RIGHT OUT!
OH MY!
NOT TO WORRY, SWEETIE. I HAVE JUST THE TICKET--

SCALP MASSAGE!
KLAK
KLAK
KLAK
KLAK
KLAK

AH YES... HOW REFRESHING!
STIMULATES THE HAIR FOLLICLES EVERY TIME!

WHY, INDEED! I FEEL SOMETHING GROWING ALREADY!
ZZIP

HEH HEH HEH! THAT GUY GIVES A WHOLE NEW MEANING TO "THE VOID OF SPACE."

URK!
YOU DID USE TOO MUCH! JUST LOOK AT MY CRANIUM. THERE'S NOTHING THERE!

COULDN'T AGREE MORE, DOC. CUSTOMER'S ALWAYS RIGHT, I SAY!
INDEED! REMEDY THIS IMMEDIATELY!

THIS 'DO WILL DO WONDERS FOR YOU, SWEETIE. IT WOIKED FOR SHIRLEY TEMPLE!
OOO, I HAVE ALL HER ALBUMS!

NOW YOU LET THAT SET, DARLING. CAN I GET YOU A CAPPUCCINO?
OH, YES, PLEASE. DECAF.

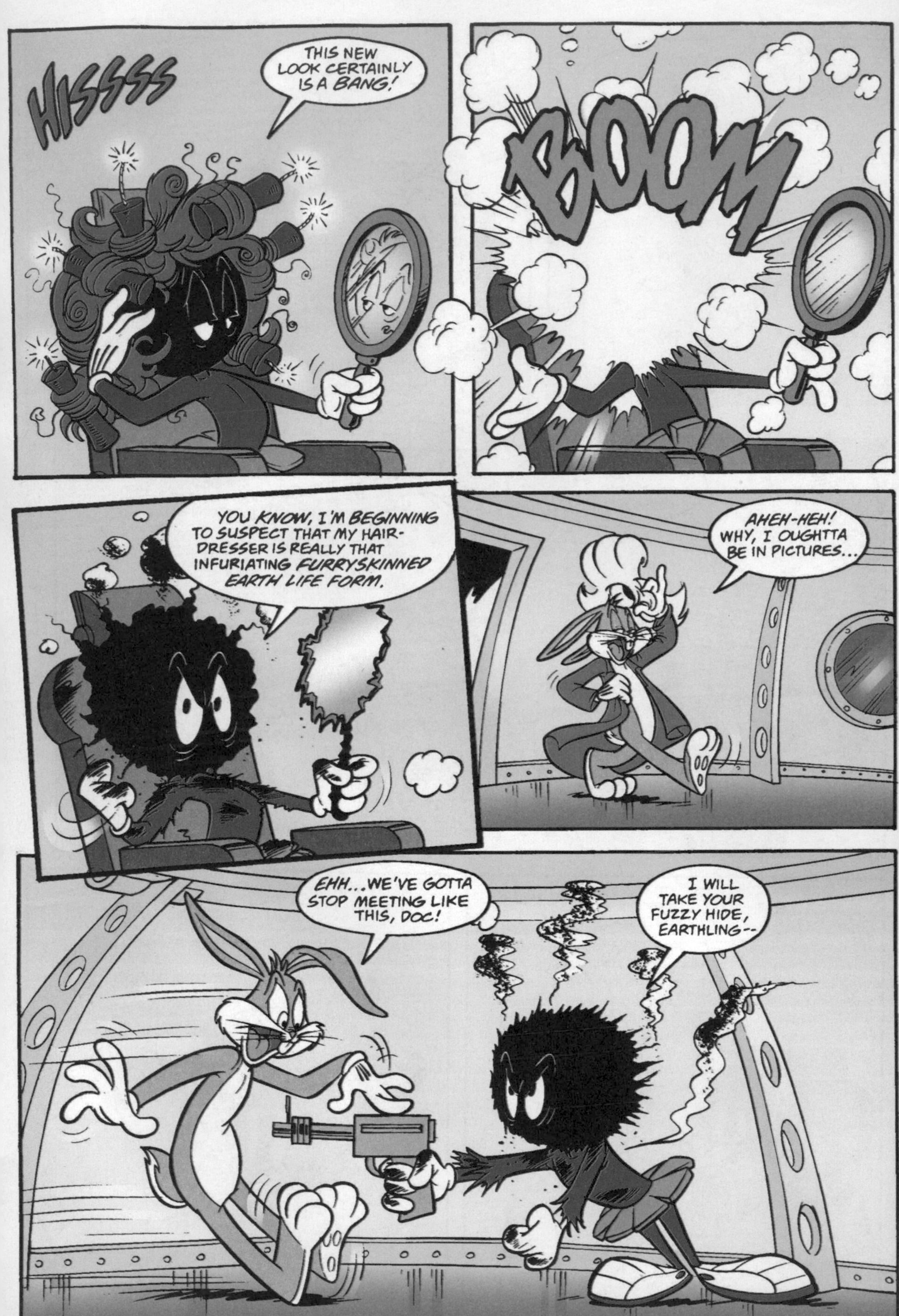
HISSSS
THIS NEW LOOK CERTAINLY IS A BANG!
BOOM
YOU KNOW, I'M BEGINNING TO SUSPECT THAT MY HAIR-DRESSER IS REALLY THAT INFURIATING FURRYSKINNED EARTH LIFE FORM.
AHEH-HEH! WHY, I OUGHTTA BE IN PICTURES...
EHH...WE'VE GOTTA STOP MEETING LIKE THIS, DOC!
I WILL TAKE YOUR FUZZY HIDE, EARTHLING--

--MEDIUM, RARE, OR WELL-DONE!
ZZRAK

ZZRAK

ZZRAK
ZZK
!

WATCH IT WITH THAT T'ING, DOC, YA ALMOST HIT ME!
ZZRAK

MUDDER!
BOOOOM!
GRACIOUS!

VWOOSH
SHOOOOSH
VWOOOM
AAAAA!!!
THIS NEVER WOULD HAVE HAPPENED HAD YOU SIMPLY SURRENDERED YOUR HAIR IN THE FIRST PLACE!
AH, SHADDUP!
AAAAA!!!

VROOOOMOOOO
BASH
EARTH! MWAH! MWAH!
GOODNESS, IT IS DREADFULLY HOT! THIS IS ALL YOUR FAULT!
SOME PEOPLE ARE JUST NEVER SATISFIED!
ZZZAK
That's All, Folks!

Writer: Terry Collins Penciller: Nelson Luty Inker: Jim Amash Letterer: John Costanza Colors: Prismacolor

WB1550

THSPARE ME THE DRAMATICSTH, SON! NOW GET CRACKIN'! THERE'STH LAUNDRY TO DO.

I HAVE A MUCH BETTER IDEA, FATHER--
--YOU DO THE LAUNDRY, AND I'LL DO THE DISHES!

WHAT, THSUDDENLY YOU'RE THSCARED OF LAUNDRY?
N-NO-- OF THE G-G-GHOST!

GHOST?! ARE YOU A CHICKEN OR A CAT, THSON? THERE'STH NO THSUCH THING ASTH GHOSTSTH! NOW MARCH!
B-BUT, FATHER--

THE ONLY "BUT" I WANNA HEAR ABOUT IS YOURS-- PARKED IN FRONT OF THE WASHING MACHINE!
sigh YES, FATHER.
ACME

SKRATCH SKRATCH
OH FATHER!! THE GHOST! THE GHOST!
SOAP

THERE'STH YOUR THSPOOK, THSON-- A COMMON MOUSTH!
SOAP
OH FATHER, I'M SO ASHAMED. ARE YOU GOING TO CATCH THE MOUSE?

WE'LL BOTH CATCH HIM-- AFTER YOU DO THE CHORESTH.
OH, BOY! YES, SIR!

OH, FATHER IS SO BRAVE! I SHOULD HAVE LISTENED TO HIM WHEN HE SAID THERE WAS NO SUCH THING AS GHOSTS!
AUSTRALIA
HOP!

HUH?
ACME DELIVERY
HOP!
I COULDA SWORN I HAD ANOTHER PACKAGE FOR THE ZOO BACK HERE!

I'M SO EMBARRASSED! MY FATHER MUST BE SO ASHAMED!
CRASH
!
SOAP

A-ALL RIGHT, MOUSE! YOU COME OUTTA THERE RIGHT NOW! I'M NOT SCARED OF YOU!
AUSTRALIA

GAAHHHHH!

OUT OF WASHING DETERGENT ALREADY?!
SLAM!
THE G-G-GHOST, FATHER! THE GHOST! I SAW HIM!

YOU'RE BEING RIDICU-LOUSTH! I'M GONNA PROVE TO YOU THERE'S NO GHOST ONCE AND FOR ALL!
DO BE CAREFUL, FATHER!

OKAY, MISTHTER MOUSE...
COME OUT COME OUT WHEREVER YOU ARE!

GOTCHA!

GAAAAAH!
G-GUH-GUH-- GHOST!

THAT'S IT, FATHER! YOU GET 'IM! SHOW THAT MOUSE WHO'S BOSS!
WHACK
TINKLE
KA-THUD
WHUNK

THSON, WHY DIDN'T YOU TELL ME THERE'S A GHOST DOWN THERE?

THERE'S A GHOST, THSON! A BIG GHOST! A BIG, NOT VERY FRIENDLY GHOST!
OH, REALLY, FATHER...

IT'S NOT VERY NICE OF YOU TO MAKE FUN OF ME! THERE'S NO NEED TO PRETEND ON MY BEHALF.
WE BOTH KNOW THERE'S NO SUCH THING AS GHOSTS! RIGHT?
UH, YEAH. NO GHOSTS. RIGHT.

THAT'S RIGHT! NO GHOSTSTH! JUST A HUGE WHITE MOUSTH ON THSTEROIDS...!
AND WHAT HAVE YOU ALWAYS TOLD ME CATS DO WITH MICE?

WE EAT 'EM UP AND THSPIT OUT THE WHISKERSTH!
THAT'S MY POP!

THERE YOU ARE, YOU THSTUPID NON-GHOST! I'LL TEACH YOU TO THSCARE MY BOY, YOU OVERGROWN CHEESE-EATER!

DON'T MAKE ME GET--
WUMP

BAPPITY BAPPITY BAPPI

...ROUGH...
HEY, WHERE'D YOU GO? I GOT THSOMETHIN' THAT'LL KNOCK YOU RIGHT ON YOUR BOUNCING BEHIND...

...OH THERE YOU ARE! HEY, WHERE'D YOUR FRIEND COME FROM?

TH-PACK
PUNCH!
BONG!
DIDJA GET HIM, FATHER? DIDJA GET THE GHOST MOUSE?
YOU BET, SONNY BOY. AND NOW TO FINISH HIM OFF!

POW!

WHAM
!

THERE YOU ARE! YOU GAVE ME A FRIGHT, LI'L GUY--I THOUGHT YOU WERE GONE FOR GOOD!
HOP!

WHY, THAT MEAN OL' MOUSE BULLY! NOBODY DOES THAT TO MY OLD MAN--
--GEE, I GUESS THE GIANT MOUSE SPLIT! MY POP MUSTA BEEN TOO MUCH TO HANDLE AFTER ALL!
ACME
LIVER

BUT I'M TELLING YOU, THE BASEMENT ISN'T HAUNTED--
LAUNDROMAT
FIS

--THERE'S NO SUCH THING AS GHOSTS!
THSAYS YOU! NOW GO GET THSOME MORE QUARTERSTH FOR THE WASHTHING MACHINE!
That's All, Folks!

WB1566
I FOOLED U.
OVER 1 BILLION GRADUATED
PULL HARDER, AL! THIS IS THE FINAL DELIVERY OF THE DAY!
DAH, I'M PULLIN', I'M PULLIN'!
DIS TASMANIAN CRATE SURE IS HEAVY! AND LOUD!
$%# @!!!

CAREFUL! LAST CRATE DELIVERED TO THIS LAB ATE THE DELIVERY-MAN ALIVE!
CHEE! NAMETAG AN' ALL?
$%# @!!
ATOMIC CLASS NIGHT BRING YOUR OWN BOMB
LABORATORY
VICIOUS PREDATOR INSIDE
DO NOT FEED
DANGER

GOSH, BOB, DERE'S NO ONE HERE!
WHERE'S THAT NUTTY PROFESSOR TA SIGN FER THIS?
COOKING WITH ATOMS
BIOLOGY FOR IDIOTS
BOB
AL

NEVER MIND! HE CAN FAX US!
$&# @%!!!
CRUNCH

The Devil and Dr. Webster

Writer
TERRY COLLINS
pencils
DAVID ALVAREZ
inks
MIKE DeCARLO
letters
JOHN COSTANZA
colors
DAVE TANGUAY

% &#@ YEEARGH SNARGL BLAZ!!!
TINK
SMASH
TINK

UH? BUT-TONS?
VID-E-O GAME?!?

BEEP!
ZORTCH

:$%# RRGLE... GAME...OV-ER...
BUMP

9%
8
2+2
BLOOSH
?!?
% $#$ ARRGGGLE!!

WHEEEEET!

BZOING

HOOOOOT!

BURP!
&%^$#!! AHHH! TAZ FEEL FRESH AND MINTY!

YOO-HOO! PRO-FES-OR WEBSTER! WHAT ARE YOU STILL DOING IN HERE?
?

OH, YOU POOR TOR-MENTED GENIUS!
ONCE AGAIN YOU'VE TRASHED YOUR LAB--AND YOUR CLOTHES!
LUCKILY, I, YOUR ASSISTANT, SEE PAST YOUR BRUTISH EXTE-RIOR AND INTO YOUR GENTLE SOUL!
I JUST KNOW ONE DAY YOU'LL RETURN MY AFFECTIONS!

COME NOW, SWEETUMS, LET'S GET INTO OUR SUIT FOR OUR BIG PRESENTATION!
$%#@ "PRE-SEN-TAY-SHUN?"

JUST LOOK AT THE TIME! WE'RE ALREADY LATE!
YUM!

OH, hee hee! PROFESSOR! YOU BEAST, YOU!
?
NO TIME FOR FLIRTING NOW! WE'LL CELEBRATE LATER!

INTO YOUR NICE SUIT--

--AND AWAY WE GO!
$%#@ TUMMY ACHE!
YOU DO LOOK OFF-COLOR! BUT ONWARD, PROFESSOR-- WE'VE GOT A GRANT TO WIN!
DOCTOR WEBSTER

GAD! MY PRESENTATION'S IN FIVE MINUTES-- AND MY FORMULA STILL DOESN'T WORK!
I MUST CALL IT OFF! I ONLY ARRANGED IT TO KEEP THAT ANNOYING LOVESTRUCK ASSISTANT OFF MY BACK!

DAH, THERE HE IS!
THAT'S HIM, MR. GAME OFFICIAL. I'D RECOGNIZE THAT HAIRY BEAST FROM TASMANIA ANYWHERE!
THIS TRANK DART'LL TAKE CARE OF HIM!

YE-OWTCH! WHAT THE--
POINK

HEY, WHERE'D HE GET THE SUIT?
DAHH, MAYBE HE ATE A SCIENTIST...?
WHATEVER. JUST GET HIM INTO THE LAB BEFORE WE GET BLAMED FOR THIS.
ZZZ

OH, THE VICIOUS WILD ANIMAL WE ORDERED HAS ARRIVED! THANK YOU SO MUCH!
DAH, DON'T MENTION IT...
GRAB
WUMP

SCIENTIFIC GENIUSES OF THE WORLD-- THANK YOU FOR COMING!
AND WITHOUT FURTHER ADO, HERE'S THE BRILLIANT DR. WEBSTER TO INTRODUCE HIS REVOLUTIONARY DISCOVERY!
X/Y = 100/80 x a²/b²
(SORT OF)

#$@ YEARRGH BLEARGH Blah Blah GREARG!!!

#$%% !!!
NEARGGG! &$%$##!!!
PFFFZZ!

BOO!
HISS!
HE'S LOST HIS MIND!
I CAME ALL THE WAY FROM STOCKHOLM FOR THIS?

%^$# ARRRRGKKK!!!
EVERYONE, PLEASE!
HE'S NOT A WELL MAN!

HE'S CRAZY AS A LOON! NUTS! INSANE! I ADMIT IT! EVERYONE KNOWS HE'S BEEN CRACKED FOR YEARS! HE EVEN DRINKS HIS OWN FORMULAS!
BUT HIS INTELLIGENCE FORMULA DOES WORK! I'LL PROVE IT!
ZZZ-- WHAT?!

$%#@!!! INSANE? WHO'S INSANE, YOU $#%@)--

DRINK UP, LAB RAT!
SPLOOSH

YOU UNBELIEVABLE TWIT!!! I'M GOING TO WRING YOUR NECK!
SEE! IT WORKS!
IT'S MADE THIS DUMB ANIMAL LIKE THE PROFESSOR AND MY PROFESSOR LIKE A DUMB ANIMAL!

A DUMB ANIMAL?
I BEG TO DIFFER!
DARLING! YOU'RE BACK!
GASP!
IT WORKS!

IT WORKS! IT REALLY DOES WORK! I'M A GENIUS!
YES YES, YOU TRAGICALLY TRANSFORMED NOW-GIFTED DISGUSTING WILD ANIMAL.
NOW SHUT UP AND LET ME BASK IN PRAISE WITH THE MAN I LOVE!
BRAVO! HOORAY! HOORAY!
THREE CHEERS FOR DR. WEBSTER!

DO YOU MIND?! I MUST WORK ON UNDOING THIS FORMULA IF I AM *EVER* TO RETURN TO MY NATURAL STATE!

I DON'T BELONG HERE! I'M A WILD BEAST!

YOU SURE ARE, PET! GIGGLE! CALL ME SCIENTIFIC PET NAMES, MY LITTLE AMOEBA!

UGH!

Oh yes, I think I'll stay in this cage-- for a long, long time!

The End...?

WB1531
ROBOCOOP
writer- MICHAEL EURY
penciller- HORACIO SAAVEDRA
inks- RUBEN TORREIRO
letters- JOHN COSTANZA
colors- DAVID TANGUAY
ISN'T TECHNOLOGY WONDERFUL? THEY CALL IT "THE FUTURE OF TWEETY BIRD PROTECTION!"
ACME EXPRESS
WE BREAK DELIVERY RECORDS—AND YOUR MERCHANDISE
ACME EXPRESS
ACME EXPRESS
ACME EXPRESS
I WOULDN'T NEED THIS NASTY MODERN ROBOCOOP IF YOU'D ONLY BEHAVE YOURSELF, SYLVESTER!
I WISH MY TWO BABIES WOULD GET ALONG!
NOW HOW DO YOU TURN ON THIS NEW-FANGLED CONTRAP-TION...?

Robocoop system activated. Tweety Bird is secure.
BRRRRP BOOP... BOOP... BOOP
OH!
GOODNESS, I'LL HAVE TO OPEN THAT OTHER BOX LATER. PLAY NICE...
... GRANNY HAS TO RUN OUT FOR SOME SUPPORT HOSE. I'LL BE BACK SOON.
SLAM!
SHE'STH GONE!
NOW TO GET DOWN TO BUSINESSTH-- BREAKFASTHT!
I WUDDN'T DO DAT IF I WAS YOU, PUDDY TAT.
BOOP... BOOP
ACME EXPRESS

You have entered a protected perimeter! You have five seconds to back away! 5-4-
BOOP BOOP BOOP BOOP
YOU'D BETTER WISTEN, PUDDY TAT! I'M PWOTECTED BY TECHNOWOGY!
3-2-
BOOP BOOP BOOP
TECHNOLOGY, TECHSTHMOLOGY! THAT HUNK 'A TIN IS NO MATCH FOR MY THSHARPLY HONED SKILLSTH! I'M AN EXTHPERTLY TRAINED PREDATOR!
YEEE-OWW!
-1
ZZZRRAK
I HOPE THE PUDDY WURNED HIS WESSON...
...BUT SOMEHOW I DON'T TINK SO!
MUM-MUM-MOTHER...

OH WOOK, I WAS WIGHT!
NO CAGE IS GONNA OUT-THSMART ME!
ACME EXPRESS
WE BREAK DELIVERY RECORDS-AND YOUR MERCHANDISE.
MISTER WOBOCOOP, I TAWT I TAW A PUDDY TAT!
BOOP BOOP
ACME EXPRESS
WE BREAK DELIVERY RECORDS-AND YOUR MERCHANDISE
You have violated a protected zone! Drop the Tweety Bird immediately!
BOOP-BOOP-BOOP
OOOOO! I DID! I DID! I DID TAW A PUDDY TAT!
ACME EXPRESS
AH, SHADDUP!!
URK!!
Robocoop launching defensive measure 29-C!
CRAK
SHAK
ACME

Defensive measure 29-c initiated!
BOOP-BOOP
AK!
BAD OL' PUDDY TAT!
Defensive measure 29-c successful. Tweety Bird secure!
SPRONNNGG
YAAAA!
OOO, DAT PUDDY HAS A WOT TO WEARN ABOUT TECHNOLOGY, DOESN'T HE?
KRUNTCH!

THSUFFERIN' THSUCCOTASH!
MAYBE THAT BIRD'STH RIGHT--
-- PERHAPSTH I CAN LEARN THSOMETHIN' FROM TECHNOLOGY. HEH-HEH.
You have entered a protected perimeter!
BOOP-BOOP BOOP
TWEETY BIRD, PREPARE TO BE CONTHSUMED AND DIGETHSTED!
OOO, HE'S TWYING IT AGAIN, MISTAH WOBOCOOP!
I'M READY FOR YA THISTH TIME, BUTHSTER! HIT ME WITH YOUR BETHST SHOT!
POING POING
As a repeat offender, your warning time has been decreased to three seconds! 3-2-
BOOP-BOOP BOOP

-1! Defensive measure 44-X initiated!
BOOP-BOOP-BOOP
YOU--
--WANNA PIECE 'A ME?
JUSTHT TRY AND HIT ME--
--MISTHTER THSTATE-OF-THE-ART!
SHAK
SHAK
SHAK
SHAK
SHAK
POING
POING
POING
POING

SOON...
HEY-- ROBODOPE!
BOOP...BOOP
UH-OH! MISTAH WOBOCOOP, DAT PUDDY TAT ISN'T GIVING UP!

I'M PUTTING A THSTOP TO HIGH-TECH ATTACKSTH!
You have entered a protected perimeter!
BOOP BOOP

AW, THSTICK A THSOCK IN IT, BUSTHTER!

I'M PULLIN' THE PLUG ON THE "FUTURE OF TWEETY BIRD PROTECTION!"
MISTER WOBOCOOP, WOOK OUT!
Danger! secure perimeter compromised!
BOOP-BOOP BOOP

TIME TO GO FISH, BUSTHER!
YANK!
POP!
Power source Vio...la...ted...
-MISTAH WOBOCOOP! ARE YOU ALL WIGHT? SPEAK TO ME!
Robocoop... deacti...vated... engaging...backup...
BOOP... BOOP... BOOP
WAKE UP, MISTAH WOBOCOOP! THE BAD OL' PUDDY TAT'S GONNA EAT ME!
HEH-HEH!
ACME EXPRESS
GUESS I PUT YOUR ROBO-PAL IN HIS CYBER-PLACE, EH, TWEETY? OR THSHOULD I CALL YOU--THSUPPER?
HELP! HELP!
ACME EXPRESS

WHAT TH'--?
Security Backup activated!
BOOP BOOP
CHRATCH
GRRRRR!!
THSUFFERIN' THSUCCOTASH!
Heh Heh! THAT PUDDY DON'T KNOW TECHNOWOGY VERY WELL, DO HE?
SNARRL!!
That's all, Folks!

Bonjour, Mon ami!
AH, PARIS! LE CITY OF LIGHT, LIFE-- AND L'AMOUR!
ZE SUN, SHE HAS SET, AND NOW EET EES TIME FOR PITCHING LE WOO, NO?
AND WHEN IT COMES TO PITCHING, PEPE EES TRULY LE MAJOR LEAGUER--

EN
ZIP!
Bonjour, MY LEETLE MORSEL! ALLOW ME TO INTRODUCE MYSELF. I AM PEPE LE PEW--

--YOUR LOVER!
GAK!

ALREADY SHE GOES FOR Le trousseau FOR OUR WEDDING NIGHT?
THE PURSUIT OF L'amour BEGINS! AND PEPE IS FLEET OF FOOT!
WHOOSH

AH, HER EYE, HER LEG!
LE OPEN
Oui, Oui!

HER TAIL! HER WHISKERS!
Oui OU--
?!
GAK!

TO ONE SIDE, Mon ami. LOVE, EET EES ONLY FOR ZEE STRONG-- LIKE PEPE!
LE OPEN

Take my hand... I am ze stranger in paradise...

AHA! I SEE YOU, MY LEETLE BUNNY RABBIT!

LET US HOP DOWN THE BUNNY TRAIL OF LOVE TOGETHER!

I AM ZE BEEG CUDDLY BEAR TO HER TEDDY, NO?
Pour Le Femmes
ZOOM

BE THE FOUNDATION IN MY GARMENT, CHERIE!
EEEEEK!

LE PERVERT!
PUNT
LE OPEN
Vive la difference, eh, ami?
THUD

SHE UPS THE STAKES IN OUR GAME OF LOVE, BUT PEPE, HE DOES NOT BLUFF!

WHERE AAAARE YOU, mon petit peignoir?

I AM HIDE-AND-GO-SEEKING FOR YOU--

A-HA! I AM LE STILTED LOVER--

--NO?

Le Pervert encore!
OUF! LE AGONY OF DEFEET!

DON'T LET EET GET TO YOU, mon ami. THEY THROW ME OUT ALL ZEE TIME!
WHAM

PEPE COMES FOR YOU, MY LEETLE MERRY WIDOW!

KNOCK KNOCK, BABY DOLL! PEPE HAS COME A-COURTING!

AH, pardonne moi, LADIES! I DID NOT MEAN TO BE THE "MEN" IN YOUR "UNMENTION-ABLES"!
GASP!

EEEEK! LE SKUNK!
AH, MY REPUTATION PRECEDES ME! PLEASE, COMPOSE YOURSELF!

PERHAPS AN AUTOGRAPH WILL QUELL YOU FLIGHTY FEMMES?

AND STAY OUT!
ZEY ALWAYS HURT THE ONES ZEY LOVE, NO?
ZEN ZEY TRULY ADORE ME, mon frere!

WHEW!

Voilà, cheri! L'amour KNOWS NO SHAME!
Vive le subterfuge!

I LOOK GOOD, NO?

Lingerie
WAIT, MY BASHFUL BUSTIER!
DO NOT BE INTIMIDATED BY MY RAVISHING BEAUTY!
Le Flowers
OH LA LA!!!

HAVE NO FEAR, CHERIE--
--I'M YOURS!
!

Zut alors! TRULY, L'amour IS A DRAG--
--NO?
Le End

Mac & Tosh "MIND YOUR MANNERS!" in THE DEVIL'S DICTION

WB1577

Writers: S. Carolan & J. Moore Pencils: Pablo Zamboni Inks: Scott McRae Letters: John Costanza Color: Bernie Mirault

Mac & Tosh "MIND YOUR MANNERS!" in POLITE PRE-REEK-QUISITES

WB1578

Writers: S. Carolan & J. Moore Pencils: Pablo Zamboni Inks: Scott McRae Letters: John Costanza Color: Bernie Mirault

Mac & Tosh "MIND YOUR MANNERS!" in FOPS & ROBBERS

WB1580

Writers: S. Carolan & J. Moore Pencils: Pablo Zamboni Inks: Scott McRae Letters: John Costanza Color: Bernie Mirault

Mac & Tosh "MIND YOUR MANNERS!" in CAT D'ETAT

WB1581

GWACIOUS ME! SOMEBODY SAVE ME FWOM THIS BAD OL' PUDDY-TAT!
OW! OW! OW! OW! OW! OW!
WHAM WHAM WHAM

IN THE NAME OF MARTHA STEWART-- STOP!!!
?

WHAT ON EARTH ARE YOU THINKING!? YOUR ACTIONS ARE JUST ABOMINABLE!
YES, YES! SIMPLY ABOMINABLE! I MUST CONCUR!
OH THANK YOU, LI'L GOPHERTH! :SNIFF:!

ARE YOU A TWEETY-BIRD-- OR AN ORANGUTAN?
QUITE RIGHT! STRAIGHTEN THAT BACK! LOOSEN THOSE ARMS! AND FOR HEAVEN'S SAKE, EXTEND THOSE PINKIES!

GEE WILLIKERS! T'ANKS FOR THE HINTS!
OH THINK NOTHING OF IT... CONTINUE!
YES, YES! BY ALL MEANS, DO PROCEED!

AND SO, A TRAVESTY OF TASTELESSNESS IS TRANSFORMED INTO A TWEETY-BIRD TRIUMPH, THANKS TO ETIQUETTE!
UNTIL NEXT TIME, GENTLE READERS, REMEMBER-- "A BIRD IN THE HAND IS NOT A PROPER SHOWER GIFT!" CIAO!

Writers: S. Carolan & J. Moore Pencils: Pablo Zamboni Inks: Scott McRae Letters: John Costanza Color: Bernie Mirault

Mac & Tosh "MIND YOUR MANNERS!" in PLANETARY PLEASANTRIES

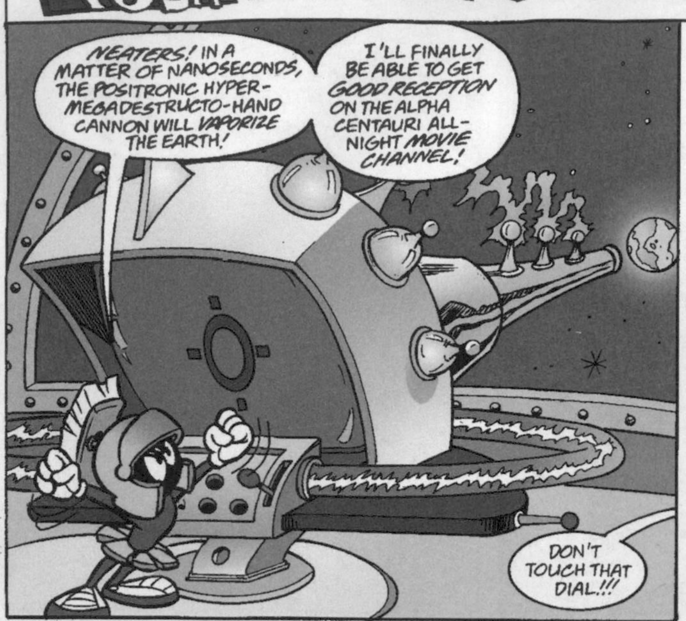

NEATERS! IN A MATTER OF NANOSECONDS, THE POSITRONIC HYPER-MEGADESTRUCTO-HAND CANNON WILL VAPORIZE THE EARTH!
I'LL FINALLY BE ABLE TO GET GOOD RECEPTION ON THE ALPHA CENTAURI ALL-NIGHT MOVIE CHANNEL!
DON'T TOUCH THAT DIAL!!!

WB1582
DO I KNOW YOU?
MY GOOD MARTIAN, YOU CERTAINLY DON'T KNOW MANNERS!
OH, QUITE! AND A NICE SEGUE, TOO, TOSH OLD BOOT!

Writers: S. Carolan & J. Moore Pencils: Pablo Zamboni Inks: Scott McRae Letters: John Costanza Color: Bernie Mirault

YOU'RE TOO KIND!
MERELY STATING FACT, OLD CHAP!
SHALL WE CONTINUE?
OH, AFTER YOU!

AS I WAS SAYING BEFORE I WAS SO POLITELY INTER-RUPTED--
THANK YOU!
--NOTHING IS MORE UNWELCOME THAN AN UNINVITED VAPORIZATION! WHAT WOULD EARTHLINGS THINK, HM?
OH, DEAR! I HADN'T THOUGHT OF THAT!

WE DO RECOMMEND HAND-ENGRAVED INDIVIDUALLY ADDRESSED GREETING CARDS.
WE TOOK THE LIBERTY OF BRINGING THE NAMES AND ADDRESSES OF 5.8 BILLION OH-SO-INTIMATE FRIENDS.
OH, THEN I'D BEST GET CRACKING!

Marvin The Martian
Requests the pleasure of your company at
The Destruction of Planet Earth
Formal attire requested
R.S.V.P.

AND SO, A MALADROIT MARTIAN IS SPARED EMBARRASSMENT, AND EARTH AVOIDS THE APOCALYPSE, THANKS TO ETIQUETTE!
UNTIL NEXT TIME, GENTLE READERS, THIS IS MAC AND TOSH REMINDING YOU: "TO BOLDLY GO" IS A SPLIT INFINITIVE! GOOD NIGHT!

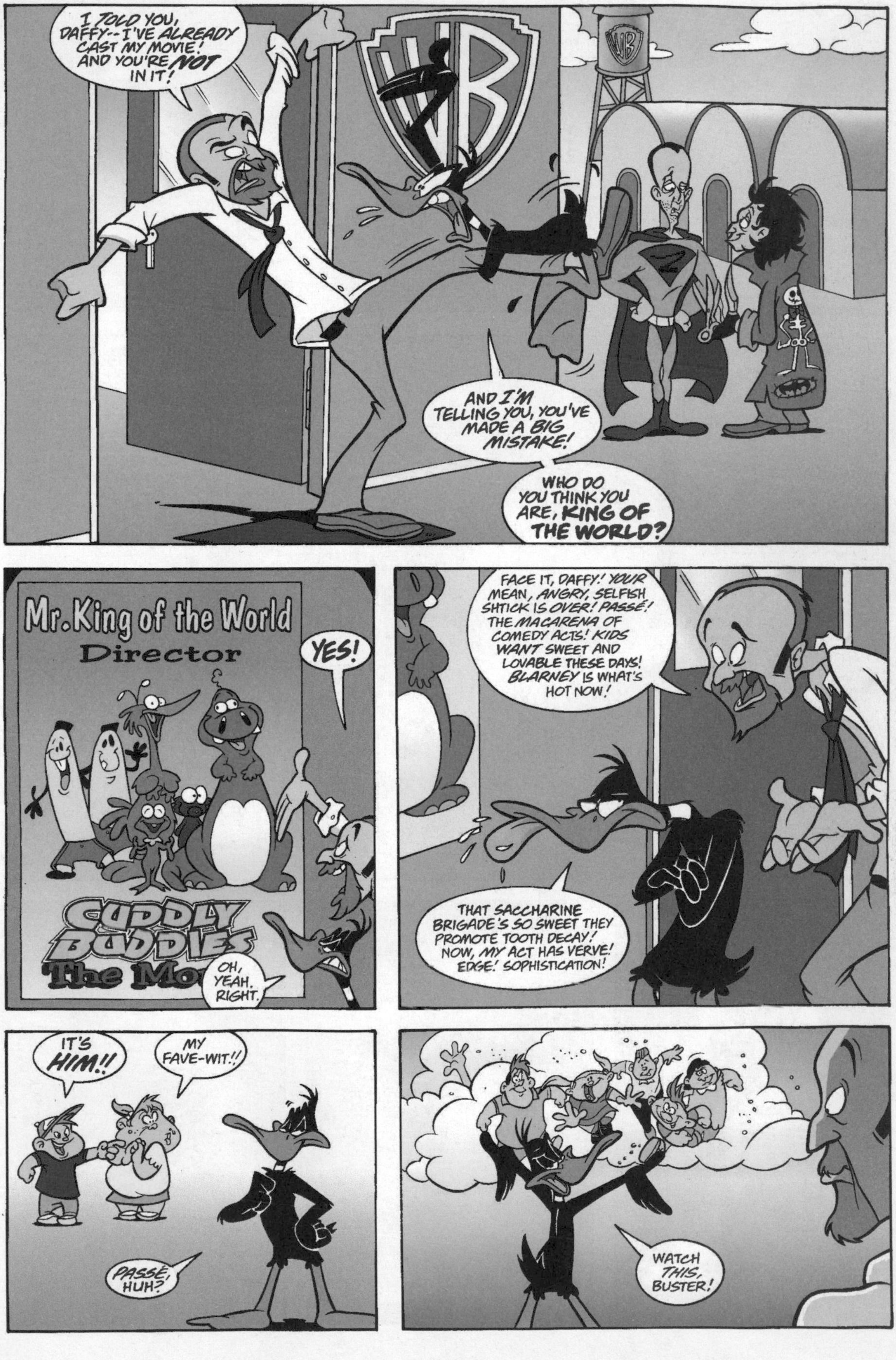

I TOLD YOU, DAFFY-- I'VE ALREADY CAST MY MOVIE! AND YOU'RE NOT IN IT!

AND I'M TELLING YOU, YOU'VE MADE A BIG MISTAKE!

WHO DO YOU THINK YOU ARE, KING OF THE WORLD?

BLARNEY!!!

WB1576

Puppet Regime

writer: MICHAEL EURY
pencils: DAVID ALVAREZ
inks: JIM AMASH
letters: JOHN COSTANZA
colors: BERNIE MIRAULT

TOP O' THE MORNIN', KIDDIES!

GOODY! SOMEONE'S SENT US A GIFT!
THAT'S 'CAUSE WE'RE GONNA BE MOVIE STARS!
BANANAS 'IN BERMUDAS™
A
B
SPECIAL DELIVERY

RRRR-RAHRR!!
EEEK!!!
A
B

HA! I'VE NEVER SEEN BANANAS SPLIT SO FAST!

THAT OUGHTTA LESSEN THEIR CUTESY-SCHMUTESY AP--

!
SHLIP!

KWAM!
--PEAL.

ABC
SUNFLOWER STREET
GROCERY
TOMATO SOUP $35.00 "I" IS FOR INFLATION
HAPPY HOUR EVERY NIGHT
V IS FOR... VIOLIN...
...VALENTINE...
...VEGETABLE...
...AND VICE PRESI-DENT!
SOMETIMES I GET THE LAST TWO MIXED UP! Tee-hee!
AL GORE
AND DON'T FORGET-- VIOLATION!
I'M FROM THE HEALTH DEPARTMENT, AND YOU SCHMUPPETS ARE A PUBLIC HEALTH THREAT!
SUGAR TOAST
DEAR ME, WHAT DID WE DO?
YOUR NAUSEA-INDUCING NICENESS ASIDE, YOUR CARPET-COVERED HIDES ARE COVERED WITH DUST!
KOFF KOFF!
YOU'VE EVEN GOT A GUY SLEEPIN' IN A TRASH CAN!
I'VE GOTTA SHUT YOU DOWN.
ZZZZZZZ
PLEASE GIVE US A CHANCE TO CLEAN UP!
WELL... ALL RIGHT. NEVER LET IT BE SAID THAT I'M NASTY OR PETTY.
OH, THANK YOU, THANK YOU!
I EVEN HAVE THE PERFECT TOOL...

--A VACUUM!
"V" IS FOR VANISH! VAMOOSE! VAMINOS!
Acme SUX-DELUX
IT'S NOT EASY BEING CLE-E-E-AN!

BLARNEY
NOW TO KISS THE BLARNEY STONE-- GOODBYE!
You're my Friend, I'm Yours too...

GOSH AND BEGORRA! 'TIS DAFFY DUCK!
BLAR
YEAH YEAH YEAH, HEY THERE, WHATEVER.
LISTEN, BLARNEY, WE GOTTA TALK. YOUR CUTE, LOVABLE SHTICK IS OVER. KIDS WANT DARK. THEY WANT ANGST. THIS IS THE '90S, PAL!

'TIS HORRIBLE NEWS! WHAT'LL I DO?
LEAVE IT TA ME, PAL. I'LL TAKE CARE OF YA.

OH YEAH, I'LL TAKE CARE OF HIM-- PERMANENTLY!
SAINTS BE PRAISED! YOU'RE SUCH A FRIEND, DAFFY. LET ME GIVE YA A HUG!

OOPSIE!
UH...

SURE 'N I MUST HAVE TRIPPED OVER A FOUR-LEAF CLOVER!
WAK!
LUCKY ME!

LESSON NUMBER ONE: QUIT BEIN' SO HAPPY! CAN'T YOU FROWN?
BUT A FROWN IS A SMILE TURNED UPSIDE-DOWN!
LOOK, I FROWN ALL THE TIME AND I'M JUST DANDY. GOT IT?

SEE? IT'S EASY!
GRR!
I'M BIG AND MEAN!
AND GREEN!

NOW TRY THIS: "THE RAIN IN SPAIN MAKES ME WANT TO COMPLAIN."
BUT I LIKE THE RAIN. IT MAKES THE FLOWERS GROW.
The RAIN IN SPAIN MAKES ME WANT TO COMPLAIN

LOOK, STUPIDSAURUS, IT'S MY WAY OR NEXT STOP EXITSVILLE, GOT IT?!
GEE, DAFFY, YOU DON'T HAVE TO BE SO CRANKY!

CRANKY PEOPLE AREN'T HAPPY PEOPLE!
AND WHEN PEOPLE AREN'T HAPPY, I GET MAD!
I THINK YOU'VE GOT IT. YOU CAN STOP NOW.
HELP!

NOW I'M REALLY IN A BAD MOOD-- AND IT'S 3 HOURS TO NAPPY TIME!
YES!
SOON THE FAME, THE GLORY, THE MERCHANDISING WILL ALL BE MINE, MINE, MINE!!

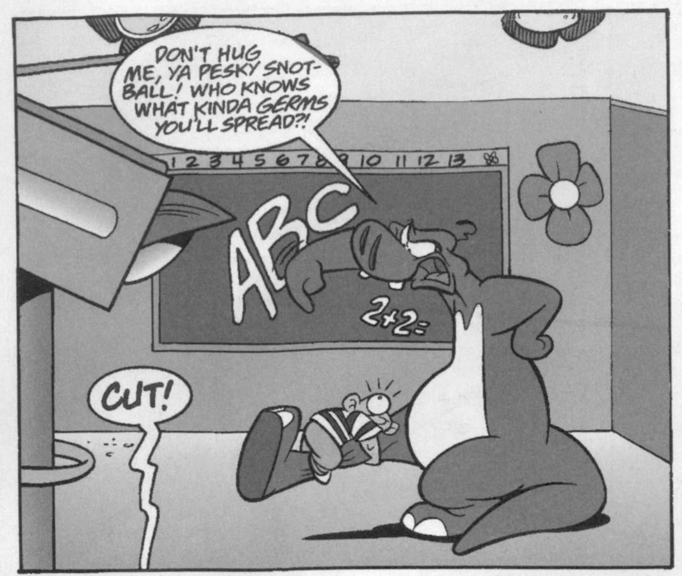
DON'T HUG ME, YA PESKY SNOT-BALL! WHO KNOWS WHAT KINDA GERMS YOU'LL SPREAD?!
CUT!
1 2 3 4 5 6 7 8 9 10 11 12 13
ABC
2+2=

WHAT'S THE BIG IDEA, STEPPIN' ON MY LINES?!!
WHAT'S UP, BLARNEY? YOU'RE NOT SWEET-- YOU'RE MEAN, ANGRY, SELFISH!
CUDDLY BUDDIES THE MOVIE
HEH HEH!

I LOVE IT!
YOU'VE GOT VERVE! EDGE! SOPHISTICATION! YOU'LL BE A SMASH!
WHAT?!

DAFFY, YOU COULD LEARN SOMETHING FROM BLARNEY, HERE!
IF YOU DON'T, WE'LL BE GLAD TO TEACH YOU!
BUT...
BUT...
BUT...

GRRR!
IS THIS WHAT THEY CALL "PUPPET" LOVE?
YIPE!
That's all, Folks!

LOONEY TUNES #42
by Peter Tumminello
& Mike DeCarlo
ARRIBA! ARRIBA! ANDALÉ!
Peter Tumminello
MIKE DeCARLO
WB1573

LOONEY TUNES #43
by David Alvarez
& Mike DeCarlo
MAGIC
IN
10
EASY
STEPS
David Alvarez
Mike DeCarlo

LOONEY TUNES #44
by David Alvarez
& Mike DeCarlo

LOONEY TUNES #45
by David Alvarez
& Mike DeCarlo
MUDDER

LOONEY TUNES #46
by David Alvarez
& Mike DeCarlo